ROGUE WAVE

A killer wave, known to mariners as a "rogue wave," was approaching a desolate area of Baja California below Ensenada. It had been born off the east coast of Australia during a violent storm; it had traveled almost 7,000 miles at a speed of 20.83 miles an hour. It was a little over 800 feet in length and measured about 48 feet from the bottom of its trough to its crest. On its passage across the Pacific, it had already killed thirteen people . . .

It was one of those perfect days to be out, Sully thought; the three Dacron sails belayed and whispering; white bow waves singing pleasant songs as the fiberglass hull, tilting to starboard, sliced though the ocean . . .

As he was about to complete a northeast tack, Sully's attention was drawn to a squadron of seagulls diving on small fish, and he did not see the giant wave that had crept up silently behind the *Sea Dog.* But a split second before it lifted the boat like a carpenter's chip, he sensed something behind him and glanced backward, toward the towering wall of shining water . . .

ROGUE WAVE

AND OTHER RED-BLOODED SEA STORIES

THEODORE TAYLOR

AN AVON FLARE BOOK

"Hauling Gold" was first published as "The Man Who Hated the Bank of South Africa" in the December 1967 issue of *Argosy Magazine*.

"Wingman, Fly Me Down!" was first published in the July 1952 issue of *Argosy Magazine*. It is based on an actual incident, though the names of the participants have been changed to protect their privacy.

"Hating Hansen" was first published as "Overboard" in the December 1952 issue of *Our Navy Magazine*.

"The Schoolie" was first published as "Cajun's Storm" in the March 1965 issue of *Argosy Magazine*.

"The 'O Tannenbaum' Affair" was first published as "The Greensleeves Affair" in the June 1964 issue of *Argosy Magazine*.

AVON BOOKS
A division of
The Hearst Corporation
1350 Avenue of the Americas
New York, New York 10019

Copyright © 1996 by Theodore Taylor
Published by arrangement with Harcourt Brace & Company
Visit our website at **http://www.AvonBooks.com**
Library of Congress Catalog Card Number: 96-14585
ISBN: 0-380-72938-5

First Avon Flare Printing: April 1998

AVON FLARE TRADEMARK REG. U.S. PAT. OFF. AND IN OTHER COUNTRIES, MARCA REGISTRADA, HECHO EN U.S.A.

Printed in the U.S.A.

WCD   10 9 8 7 6 5 4 3 2 1

For Sean Michael Taylor—
wonderful, rambunctious, scalawag grandson

Contents

ROGUE WAVE

AND OTHER RED-BLOODED SEA STORIES

Introduction

I fell in love with the sea from a position on land. As a boy of twelve, in a little tidewater Virginia town, I would lie in bed and listen to the ships' whistles and horns on the Elizabeth River. I was sure the vessels, sailing on the night tide, were bound for exotic ports around the world. I wanted to be aboard them, to be a sailor, to travel to London and Conakry and Hong Kong and the Java Sea.

The first time I saw the Atlantic Ocean was a year earlier, on a Sunday afternoon at Virginia's Cape Henry, at the mouth of the Chesapeake Bay. While I was on the beach that winter day, Coast Guardsmen took a lifesaving boat out through the surf, ten of them pulling on long-sweep Viking oars—an unforgettable sight.

Many times I rode my bike into nearby Portsmouth and sat on a piling at the Isaac Fass fish dock to watch the unloading of all sorts of catches. At about the same time, my father helped me build a rowboat and I used it to crab for blues in Cradock's Paradise Creek and the Elizabeth.

He also bought an old, beat-up boat for fifty dollars. It was powered with an ancient two-cycle gasoline up-and-downer, started by jerking the flywheel. We fished the waters of busy Hampton Roads and I watched the ships come by us, in- and outbound, and longed to be on their decks.

That dream came true during World War II, on merchant ships. Frightened sleepless on many nights, I sailed the torpedo waters of the North Atlantic, the Gulf of Mexico, and the Caribbean as an able-bodied seaman, deck cadet, and third mate. In 1944, I was called to active duty in the navy and served on two ships in the Pacific.

Despite occasional foul weather, and the torpedo waters, my love for the sea did not falter. For every bad day, there were wondrous days and nights on the bridges of all the ships—serene days when the waters smiled, and nights when every star in the universe seemed to be over my head.

I live at the beach now, and when the tides allow, walk it every day with my wife and my dog. When I have to walk the streets instead, the day is somehow incomplete. During the summer I fish out of Dana Point with an old friend, Ray Johnson. We seldom catch very much, but just to be out on the water, away from traffic and noise, is a sweet reward.

My first love is my extended family and grandchildren, but my second love is always the sea, an affair that began almost three-quarters of a century ago. So I wrote these stories.

THEODORE TAYLOR
LAGUNA BEACH, CALIFORNIA
1996

Rogue Wave

A killer wave, known to mariners as a "rogue wave," was approaching a desolate area of Baja California below Ensenada. It had been born off the east coast of Australia during a violent storm; it had traveled almost 7,000 miles at a speed of 20.83 miles an hour. Driven by an unusual pattern of easterly winds, it was a little over 800 feet in length and measured about 48 feet from the bottom of its trough to its crest. On its passage across the Pacific, it had already killed thirteen people, mostly fishermen in small boats, but also an entire French family of five aboard a 48-foot schooner . . .

Melissa "Scoot" Atkins went below into the *Old Sea Dog*'s tiny galley, moving down the three steps of the companionway, closing the two solid entry doors behind her, always a good idea in offshore sailing. The three horizontal hatch boards that were on top of the doors were also firmly in place, securing the 30-foot Baba type against sudden invasion of seawater.

*   *   *

Rogues and sneakers have been around since the beginning of the oceans, and the earliest sea literature makes note of "giant" waves. The U.S. Navy manual Practical Methods for Observing and Forecasting Ocean Waves *says, "In any wave system, after a long enough time, an exceptional high one will occur. These monstrous out-sized waves are improbable but still possible and the exact time of occurrence can never be predicted." Naval hydrography studies indicate that waves 15 to 25 feet high qualify for "sneaker" or "sleeper" status; the freak rogue is up to 100 feet or over. As waters slowly warm they seem to be occurring more frequently. In 1995 the* Queen Elizabeth 2, *the QE2 the great British passenger liner, encountered a 95-foot rogue south of Newfoundland. More than 900 feet long, the QE2 rode over it, but her captain said it looked like they were sailing into the White Cliffs of Dover.*

Sullivan Atkins, Scoot's oldest brother, was steering the cutter-rigged boat on a northerly course about 15 miles off desolate Cabo Colnett, south of Ensenada. Under a brilliant sun, the glittering blue Pacific rose and fell in long, slick swells, a cold light breeze holding steady.

Below deck Scoot was listening to Big Sandy & His Fly-Rite Boys doing "Swingin' West," and singing along with them while slicing leftover steak from last night's meal. They'd grilled it on a small charcoal ring that was mounted outboard on the starboard side at the stern, trailing sparks into the water.

The *Sea Dog* had every blessed thing, including a barbecue pit, she marveled.

Scoot was learning how to be a deep-water sailor. She was fourteen years old and pretty, with dark hair. Though small in size, not even five feet, she was strong. She'd started off with eight-foot Sabots. On this trip, her first aboard the *Sea Dog*, she'd manned the wheel for most of the three days they'd been under way. She'd stood four-hour watches at night. Sully was a good teacher.

It was one of those perfect days to be out, Sully thought: the three Dacron sails belayed and whispering, white bow waves singing pleasant songs as the fiberglass hull, tilting to starboard, sliced through the ocean. It was a day filled with goodness, peace, and beauty. They'd come south as far as Cabo Colnett, turning back north only an hour ago. They'd sailed from Catalina Island's Avalon Harbor, the *Sea Dog*'s home port, out in the channel off Los Angeles. Sully had borrowed the boat from a family friend, Beau Tucker, a stockbroker with enough money to outfit it and maintain it properly. Built by Ta-Shing, of Taiwan, she was heavy and sturdy, with a teakwood deck and handsome teakwood interior, and the latest in navigation equipment. Sully had sailed her at least a dozen times. He'd been around boats, motor and sail, for many of his nineteen years. He thought the *Old Sea Dog* was the best, in her category, that he'd ever piloted.

As he was about to complete a northeast tack, Sully's attention was drawn to a squadron of seagulls diving on small fish about a hundred yards off the port bow, and he did not see the giant wave that had crept up silently behind the *Sea Dog*. But a split second before it lifted the boat like a carpenter's chip, he sensed something behind him and glanced backward, toward the towering wall of shining water.

It was already too late to shout a warning to Scoot so she could escape from the cabin; too late to do anything except hang on to the wheel with both hands; too late even to pray. He did manage a yell as the *Sea Dog* became vertical. She rose up the surface of the wall stern first and then pitch-poled violently, end over end, the bow submerging and the boat going upside down, taking Sully and Scoot with it, the 40-foot mast, sails intact, now pointing toward the bottom.

Scoot was hurled upward, legs and arms flying, her head striking the after galley bulkhead and then the companionway steps and the interior deck, which was now the ceiling. She instantly blacked out.

Everything loose in the cabin was scattered around what had been the overhead. Water was pouring in and was soon lapping at Scoot's chin. It was coming from a four-inch porthole that had not been dogged securely and a few other smaller points of entry.

Sully's feet were caught under forestay sailcloth, plastered around his face, but then he managed to shove clear and swim upward, breaking water. He looked at the mound of upside-down hull, bottom to the sky, unable to believe that the fine, sturdy *Sea Dog* had been flipped like a cork, perhaps trapping Scoot inside. Treading water, trying to collect his thoughts, he yelled, ''Scoot,'' but there was no answer. Heart pounding, unable to see over the mound of the hull, he circled it, thinking she might have been thrown clear. But there was no sign of her.

He swam back to the point of cabin entry, took several deep breaths, and dove. He felt along the hatch boards and then opened his eyes briefly to see that the doors were still closed. She *was* still inside. Maneuvering his body, he pulled on the handles. The doors were jammed, and he returned to the surface for air.

He knew by the way the boat had already settled that there was water inside her. Under usual circumstances, the hull being upright, there would be four feet, nine inches of hull below the waterline. There would be about the same to the cabin overhead, enabling a six-foot-six person to walk about down there.

Panting, blowing, Sully figured there was at least a three-foot air pocket holding the *Sea Dog* on the surface, and if Scoot hadn't been knocked unconscious and drowned, she could live for quite a while in the dark chamber. How long, he didn't know.

In the blackness, water continued to lap at Scoot's chin. She had settled against what had been the deck of the galley alcove, her body in an upright position on debris. Everything not tied down or in a locker was now between the overhead ribs. Wooden hatch covers from the bilges were floating in the water and the naked bilges were exposed. Just aft of her body, and now above it, was the small diesel engine as well as the batteries. Under the water were cans of oil, one of them leaking. Battery acid might leak, too. Few sailors could imagine the nightmare that existed inside the *Sea Dog*. Scoot's pretty face was splashed with engine oil.

*   *   *

Over the next five or six minutes, Sully dove repeatedly, using his feet as a fulcrum, and using all the strength that he had in his arms, legs, and back, in an effort to open the doors. The pressure of the water defeated him. Then he thought about trying to pry the doors open with the wooden handle of the scrub brush. Too late for that, he immediately discovered. It had drifted away, along with Scoot's nylon jacket, her canvas boat shoes—anything that could float.

Finally he climbed on top of the keel, catching his breath, resting a moment, trying desperately to think of a way to enter the hull. Boats of the Baba class, built for deep-water sailing, quite capable of reaching Honolulu and beyond, were almost sea-tight unless the sailors made a mistake or unless the sea became angry. The side ports were supposed to be dogged securely in open ocean. Aside from the cabin doors, there was no entry into that cabin without tools. He couldn't very well claw a hole through the inch of tough fiberglass.

He thought about the hatch on the foredeck but it could only be opened from inside the cabin. Then there was the skylight on the top of the seventeen-foot cabin, used for ventilation as well as a sun source; that butterfly window, hinged in the middle, could be opened only from the inside. Even with scuba gear, he couldn't open that skylight unless he had tools.

He fought back tears of frustration. There was no way to reach Scoot. And he knew what would happen down there. The water would slowly and inevitably rise until the air pocket was only six inches; her head would be trapped between the surface of the water and the dirty bilge. The water would torture her, then it would drown her. Seawater has no heart, no brain. The *Sea Dog* would then drop to the ocean floor, thousands of feet down, entombing her forever.

Maybe the best hope for poor Scoot was that she was already dead, but he had to determine whether she was still alive. He began pounding on the hull with the bottom of his fist, waiting for a return knock. At the same time, he shouted her name over and over. Nothing but silence from inside there. He wished he'd hung on to the silly scrub brush. The wooden handle would make more noise than the flesh of his fist.

Almost half an hour passed, and he finally broke down and sobbed. His right fist was bloody from the constant pounding. Why hadn't *he* gone below to make the stupid sandwiches? Scoot would have been at the wheel when the wave grasped the *Sea Dog*. His young sister, with all her life to live, would be alive now.

They'd had a good brother-sister relationship. He'd teased her a lot about being pint sized and she'd teased back, holding her nose when he brought one girl or another home for display. She'd always been spunky. He'd taken her sailing locally, in the channel, but she'd wanted an offshore cruise for her fourteenth birthday. Now she'd had one, unfortunately.

Their father had nicknamed her Scoot because, as a baby, she'd crawled so fast. It was still a fitting name for her as a teenager. With a wiry body, she was fast in tennis and swimming and already the school's champion in the 100-yard dash.

Eyes closed, teeth clenched, he kept pounding

away with the bloody fist. Finally he went back into
the ocean to try once more to open the doors. He
sucked air, taking a half dozen deep breaths, and
then dove again. Bracing his feet against the companionway frames, he felt every muscle straining,
but the doors remained jammed. He was also now
aware that if they did open, more water would rush
in and he might not have time to find Scoot in the
blackness and pull her out. But he was willing to
take the gamble.

Scoot awakened as water seeped into her mouth and
nose. For a moment she could not understand where
she was; how she got there; what had happened . . .
Vaguely, she remembered the boat slanting steeply
downward, as if it were suddenly diving, and she
remembered feeling her body going up.

That's all she remembered, and all she knew at
the moment was that she had a fierce headache and
was in chill water in total darkness. It took a little
longer to realize she was trapped in the *Sea Dog*'s
cabin, by the galley alcove. She began to feel around
herself and to touch floating things. The air was
thick with an oil smell. Then she ran her hand over
the nearest solid thing—a bulkhead. *That's strange*,
she thought—her feet were touching a pot. She lifted
her right arm and felt above her—the galley range.
The galley range above her? THE BOAT WAS UPSIDE
DOWN. She felt for the companionway steps and
found the entry doors and pushed on them; that was
the way she'd come in. The doors didn't move.

Sully crawled up on the wide hull again, clinging to
a faint hope that a boat or ship would soon come by;
but the sun was already in descent, and with night

coming on, chances of rescue lessened with each long minute. It was maddening to have her a few feet away and be helpless to do anything. Meanwhile the hull swayed gently, in eerie silence.

Scoot said tentatively, "Sully?" Maybe he'd been drowned. Maybe she was alone and would die here in the foul water.

She repeated his name, but much more loudly. No answer. She was coming out of shock now and fear more icy than the water was replacing her confusion. To die completely alone? It went that way for a few desperate moments, and then she said to herself, *Scoot, you've got to get out of here! There has to be some way to get out . . .*

Sully clung to the keel with one hand, his body flat against the smooth surface of the hull. There was ample room on either side of the keel before the dead-rise, the upward slope of the hull. The *Sea Dog* had a beam of ten feet. Unless a wind and waves came up, he was safe enough in his wet perch.

Scoot again wondered if her brother had survived and if he were still around the boat or on it. With her right foot she began to probe around the space beneath her. The pot had drifted away but her toes felt what seemed to be flatware. That made sense. The drawer with the knives and forks and spoons had popped out, spilling its contents. She took a deep breath and ducked under to pick out a knife. Coming up, she held the knife blade, reaching skyward with the handle . . .

* * *

Eyes closed, brain mushy, exhausted, Sully heard a faint tapping and raised up on his elbows to make sure he wasn't dreaming. No, there was a tapping from below. He crawled back toward what he thought was the source area, the galley area, and put an ear to the hull. *She was tapping!* He pounded the fiberglass, yelling, "Scoot, Scooot, Scooot . . ."

Scoot heard the pounding and called out, "Sully, I'm here, I'm here!" Her voice seemed to thunder in the air pocket.

Sully yelled, "Can you hear me?"

Scoot could only hear the pounding.
   "Help me out of here . . ."

Ear still to the hull, Sully shouted again, "Scoot, can you hear me?" No answer. He pounded again and repeated, "Scoot, can you hear me?" No answer. The hull was too thick and the slop of the sea, the moan of the afternoon breeze, didn't help.

Though she couldn't hear his voice, the mere fact that he was up there told her she'd escape. Sully had gotten her out of jams before. There was no one on earth that she'd rather have as a rescue man than her oldest brother. She absolutely knew she'd survive.

Though it might be fruitless, Sully yelled down to the galley alcove, "Listen to me, Scoot. You'll have to get out by yourself. I can't help you. I can't break in. Listen to me, I know you're in water, and the best way out is through the skylight. You've got to dive down and open it. You're small enough to go through it . . .'' She could go through either section of the butterfly window. "Tap twice if you heard me!"

She did not respond, and he repeated what he'd just said, word for word.

No response. No taps from below.

Scoot couldn't understand why he didn't just swim down and open the doors to the cabin, release her. That's all he needed to do, and she'd be free.

Sully looked up at the sky. "Please, God, help me, help us." It was almost unbearable to know she was alive and he was unable to do anything for her. Then he made the decision to keep repeating: "Listen to me, Scoot. You'll have to get out by yourself. I can't break in. Listen to me, the best way out is through the skylight. You've got to dive down and open it. You're small enough to go through it . . .''

He decided to keep saying it the rest of the day and into the night or for as long as it took to penetrate the hull with words. *Skylight! Skylight!* Over and over.

He'd heard of mental telepathy but had not thought much about it before. Now it was the only way to reach her.

Scoot finally thought that maybe Sully was hurt, maybe helpless up on that bottom, so that was why he couldn't open the doors and let her out. That had to be the reason—Sully up there with broken legs. *So I'll have to get out on my own*, she thought.

Over the last two days, when she wasn't on the wheel she had been exploring the *Sea Dog*, and she thought she knew all the exits. Besides the companionway doors, which she knew she couldn't open, there was the hatch on the foredeck for access to the sails; then there was the skylight, almost in the middle of the long cabin. Sully had opened it, she remembered, to air out the boat before they sailed. As she clung to a light fixture by the alcove, in water up to her shoulders, something kept telling her she should first try the butterfly windows of the skylight. The unheard message was compelling—*Try the skylight*.

Sully's voice was almost like a recording, a mantra, saying the same thing again and again, directed down to the position of the galley.

Scoot remembered that an emergency flashlight was bracketed on the bulkhead above the starboard settee, and she assumed it was waterproof. From what Sully had said, Beau Tucker took great care in selecting emergency equipment. It might help to actually see the dogs on the metal skylight frame. She knew she wouldn't have much time to spin them loose. Maybe thirty or forty seconds before she'd have to surface for breath. Trying to think of the exact position of the upside-down flashlight, she again tapped on the hull to let her brother know she was very much alive.

He pounded back.

Sully looked at his watch. Almost four-thirty. About three hours to sundown. Of course, it didn't make much difference to Scoot. She was already in dank night. But it might make a difference if she got out after nightfall. He didn't know what kind of shape she was in. Injured, she might surface and drift away.

The mantra kept on.

Scoot dove twice for the boxy flashlight, found it, and turned it on, suddenly splitting the darkness and immediately feeling hopeful. But it was odd to see the *Sea Dog*'s unusual overhead, the open hatchways into the bilge and the debris floating on the shining water, all streaked with lubricants; odd to see the toilet upside down. She held the light underwater and it continued to operate.

Every so often, Sully lifted his face to survey the horizon, looking for traffic. He knew they were still within sixteen or seventeen miles of the coast, though the drift was west. There was usually small boat activity within twenty miles of the shore—fishermen or pleasure boats.

Scoot worked herself forward a few feet, guessing where the skylight might be, and then went down to find the butterfly windows, the flashlight beam cutting through the murk. It took a few seconds to locate them and put a hand on one brass dog. She tried to turn it, but it was too tight for her muscles and she rose up to breathe again.

Not knowing what was happening below or whether Scoot was trying to escape, Sully was getting more anxious by the moment. He didn't know whether or not the crazy telepathy was working. He wished she would tap again to let him know she was still alive. It had been more than twenty minutes since she'd last tapped.

* * *

Scoot had seen a toolbox under the companionway steps and went back to try and find it. She guessed there'd be wrenches inside it, unless they'd spilled out. Using the flashlight again, she found the metal box and opened it. Back to the surface to breathe again, and then back to the toolbox to extract a wrench. With each move she was becoming more and more confident.

A big sailboat, beating south, came into Sully's view; but it was more than two miles away and the occupants—unless he was very lucky—would not be able to spot the *Sea Dog*'s mound and the man standing on it, waving frantically.

Four times Scoot needed to dive, once for each dog; and working underwater was at least five times as difficult as trying to turn them in usual circumstances. She'd aim the light and rest it to illuminate the windows. Finally, all the dogs were loose and she rose once again. This time, after filling her lungs to bursting, she went down and pushed on the starboard window. It cracked a little, but the outside sea pressure resisted and she had to surface again.

Sully sat down, almost giving up hope. How long the air pocket would hold up was anybody's guess. The boat had settled at least six inches in the last two hours. It might not last into the night.

On her sixth dive Scoot found a way to brace her feet against the ceiling ribs. She pushed with all her strength, and this time the window opened. Almost out of breath, she quickly pushed her body through and the *Old Sea Dog* released her. Treading water beside the hull, she sucked in fresh air and finally called out, "Sully . . ."

He looked her way, saw the grin of triumph on the oil-stained imp face, and dived in to help her aboard the derelict.

Shivering, holding each other for warmth all night, they rode and rocked, knowing that the boat was sinking lower each hour.

Just after dawn, the *Red Rooster*, a long-range sports fishing boat out of San Diego bound south to fish for wahoo and tuna off the Revilla Gigedo Islands, came within a hundred yards of the upside-down sailboat and stopped to pick up its two chattering survivors.

The *Red Rooster*'s captain, Mark Stevens, asked, "What happened?"

"Rogue wave," said Sully. That's what he planned to say to Beau Tucker as well.

Stevens winced and nodded that he understood.

The *Old Sea Dog* stayed on the surface for a little while longer, having delivered her survivors to safety; then her air pocket breathed its last and she slipped beneath the water, headed for the bottom.

Hauling Gold

The Castle Lines usually took the Bank of South Africa's gold to England, but the SS *Kimberly Castle* was now laid up in dry dock with engine trouble; the jaunty *Good Hope Castle* was churning toward Liverpool; and the big, beautiful *Johannesburg Castle*, with its modern specie room, its vault, had not yet departed London. The Castle Lines' other ships were spread around the world, all busy.

So it was the lowly old diesel motorship *Massinga*, last of her German-built breed in East African waters, that was now reluctantly pressed into emergency service at Durban to haul the bullion to Southampton. Twenty bars in each sealed box. It came to forty-eight-plus million in British pounds, or upward of fifty-one million in U.S. dollars, in lovely, negotiable gold.

It gave the *Massinga*'s master, Harry Brand, no little satisfaction. That was hardly adequate to describe his true feelings. From his insteps to the roots of his gray curly hair, Brand was percolating inside. His wiry body was alive with the thought of his cargo. Behind a calm, his eyes burned and his palms were wet. But his monkeylike face, with its pudgy nose and furry eyebrows and weathered cheeks, was serene, masking the temptation to laugh openly. After years of dog-tailing it, he was once again whole.

In the late sixties, the cream-colored *Massinga*, a comfortable Blohm & Voss vessel of seventy-two hundred tons, with space for eighteen passengers and a very adequate specie room, had been on the bullion run to England, sharing cargoes with the powerful Castle Line. Then the Bank of South Africa, clearing its mighty throat, had hinted about the *Massinga*'s slow speed, had fretted about possible breakdowns, had made excuses about the security of the vault, and finally had issued a letter voiding the profitable contract. It had been a terrible blow to Brand.

They were all *excuses*, Brand knew. Polite ways of saying, *Captain Brand is no longer trustworthy. He drinks too much. He is often seen in bars in Durban, not to mention Port Elizabeth, Cape Town, Las Palmas, and even Liverpool. And he wrecked the Café Penguin in Lourenco Marques.*

All perfectly true twelve years ago. After his wife, Angela, and his son, Eric, were killed at a railway crossing, Captain Brand had floated his sorrow in alcohol.

But for ten years Brand hadn't so much as thumbed a cork or sniffed a wine bud. His shore visits had been as circumspect, as unbrawling, as nonalcoholic as the conduct of an aging monk. For three years it was only to prove to the Bank of South Africa that he was indeed reliable. Then it became something else, a way of honoring Angela and Eric, for the Bank of South Africa wasn't really interested in the rehabilitation of Harry Brand. They were quite happy to have the high muckety-muck Castle Lines haul *all* the gold, and the fact that, as a result, Brand had to scrounge, even beg, for cargo and passengers to England was of no concern. But for this voyage he hadn't had to scrounge; Angela and Eric would have been proud.

At this moment, Brand was observing the unique pageant taking place outside the door of the *Massinga*'s long-unused specie room. The spick-and-span white-coated, straw-hatted official from the Bank of South Africa, calling himself Chapman—someone they'd acquired recently, for he was unknown to Brand—had come to tally the gold. Brand had known his cut immediately when he'd crawled from the black sedan that led the convoy of five armored trucks. A proper gent in his midthirties, sniffy and stuffy; arrogant.

But the gold procedure had not changed. The loading was through Number 3 hatch by crane, thence into the vault room on hand dolly. Chapman stood tensely with his tally board. The witnesses, as prescribed by the bank, were Brand; Calkins, the *Massinga*'s mountainous first officer; the Afrikaner, Westmann—actually a Hollander—who was chief purser; Gopal Singh, the new third officer; and Knight, the junior purser. There were three bored armed guards in the hold, two on the deck, and three on the pier. They had automatic weapons.

Brand watched as Chapman, now sweating under his straw hat, checked the serial number of each box against his master list, making certain that none of the seals were broken. Then the boxes, following BSA demands, were stacked in the specie room so they could be visually checked each day without touch by human hand. The seals were exposed so they could be seen from the open door. All very fusty bank style.

A bit after noon, Chapman turned worriedly and said, "We'll have an overflow of two million." In pounds, of course.

Brand nodded. He'd calculated that a week ago. "I've cleared the mail room."

"No mail room has security for this, Captain Brand," Chapman said sharply.

Brand smiled back. "Mine has steel doors, sir. Would you be satisfied if they were welded?"

"Perhaps. We'll see."

Chapman went on checking the final boxes. Then they broke for lunch. The others ate in the ship's spacious teakwood officer's saloon, but Brand invited Chapman to dine in his cabin. It was customary, Brand remembered. The bank official picked at his food as if what came out of the *Massinga*'s galley was likely contaminated.

"They feed better on the Castle ships, sir?" Brand asked.

Chapman reddened. He said, "Captain Brand, except by hearsay, I know nothing about you. But to look at the *Massinga*, I feel very uncomfortable."

Brand placed a genuine smile on his monkey face. "She was a good ship, sir. Still is. Did anyone ever tell you that I carried thirty-one cargoes of bullion for your bank without loss of a bar?"

After a long silence, Chapman looked up from his mouth-roasting curry to ask, "About your officers, Captain. They've been with you for quite a while?"

"Except Singh. He's a replacement. My regular third mate, Mueller, is in a Durban hospital. Accident ashore."

Chapman grabbed this with eagerness. "What do you know about Singh?"

Brand shrugged. "He has his papers. He's qualified."

In truth, Brand knew little about Gopal Singh—other than his birthplace, Mangalore, India, and his age, twenty-three. Eric had died at twenty-three, and in some way Singh reminded Brand of his son. But though Brand didn't yet know much about Singh, he well knew Mangalore's emerald harbor, crowded with fishing boats and Arab dhows that traded gold and dates for cloth and spices. He guessed that Singh had been mud-poor. What really counted was that Mangalore men were good on ships.

Chapman sighed. "I don't like it."

Brand said cheerfully, "Then find another third officer for me, Mr. Chapman. We sail in four hours—unless you want a delay."

Chapman frowned. "If we wanted a delay, we'd wait for the *Jo'burg Castle*."

Brand held up his small, powerful hands in resignation.

"What stops do you have?" Chapman asked.

"Port Elizabeth, Mossel Bay, Cape Town, Las Palmas, then direct to Southampton."

"Why so many stops?" asked Chapman curtly.

"I have cargo to load and off-load," Brand replied. "I can't pay for the trip out of your bullion fee alone."

Chapman sighed again, and then the lunch was over and they went to the mail room. Chapman scanned it, tapped on the steel bulkheads, and came out in a jumpy state. He went to the dock, made a call to his office in Durban to discuss the two million overflow, and then returned. He was fuming. "All right, Captain. I've been overruled." He ran his fingers around the door edges and then said, "Welded sound—do you understand?" Brand nodded and used the ship's phone to summon Chief Engineer Watts.

Meanwhile the dollies were trundling in the boxes. The silent, awesome pageant continued. Brand studied his officers now and then as they stood, witnessing the loading procedures. None of them had ever carried gold, to his knowledge. They didn't know that giddy feeling. Didn't know how it was to tramp the bridge at night when below your feet was a fortune; to lie in your oven bunk and think of the yellow bars that were two hundred paces from your fingertips. Yes, these officers were in awe, and should be.

Brand also knew that once Mr. Chapman stood on the dock, once the *Massinga* cleared Durban harbor, they'd laugh nervously and banter about how the gold might be removed; they'd even plot the theft— in jest, of course.

Only once, sixteen years ago, had it gone beyond saloon jest. Beyond the bridge pacing and the imaginative thrashing in hot bunks. Greed had slithered out of the engine room in the form of a dirty Cockney oiler. He'd had an ingenious plan to steal the bullion; but the greed had ended with a single shot, placed accurately between his eyes by one Harry Brand, ship's master. For four years Brand had enjoyed a hero image with the Bank of South Africa; then came the railway crossing accident, the deaths of Angela and Eric, the drinking bouts.

Soon the spitting blue flame of a welding torch drew a thick bead around the steel door flange of the mail

room, and then the *Massinga*'s air horn tooted
hoarsely three times. Chapman stood outside the
mail room to hand, ceremoniously, a specie room
key each to Brand, First Officer Calkins, and Chief
Purser Westmann. The keys were for the daily inspection.

Brand stuck his key into his pocket and said to
Chapman, "The bullion will be safe."

The bank man coughed slightly, threw questioning
glances at Calkins and Westmann, then murmured,
"Good voyage, Captain."

He hurried off the *Massinga*.

Calkins went up to the foredeck to boss the line
handling. Westmann disappeared down the starboard
passageway to his office, and Captain Brand nimbly
climbed three inside ladders to the wheelhouse.

The *Massinga*, her diesels giving off the sound of
a thousand gravel-throated bullfrogs and shaking her
stem to stern, stood out to sea in the late-afternoon
sun: a rust-blotched ship of lines that were somewhat
startling on the Elbe River in 1955 but rather old-
fashioned anywhere in 1975. She took the first bite
of sea tiredly, and then Brand rolled her south on
the coastal shipping lane, avoiding a pair of ponderous lateen-rigged dhows that seemed not to care
about collision. It was deceptive, since the Arabs
were excellent seamen and the dhows, with their
gaily painted prows, were not quite as ponderous as
they looked.

Breathing out contentment, Brand settled in his
chair on the starboard wing, his short legs drawn up
on the rungs, again thinking what it meant to have
an absolute fortune in bullion aboard. He stayed on
the wing until he was roughly abeam of Umzinto,
considering how comparatively simple it would be

to transfer the bullion to one of the big dhows.

Then Lowe, the radio operator, hobbled up and handed him a message. It was from the Durban hospital. Third Officer Mueller was dead of head injuries. *How strange*, Brand thought.

The circumstances of Mueller's injury had bothered him for two days. A quiet, peaceful man from Bremen, the third officer had never been involved in any trouble. Yet he'd been found in a filthy part of town, battered about the head, reeking of whiskey. Trouble was, Mueller was a diabetic and didn't drink.

Captain Brand decided to dine in the officers' saloon rather than in his own quarters. He wanted to hear the table talk this night.

For the benefit of those who hadn't been outside the specie room door, Calkins was lording it up. "Can you believe it now, this grubbin' ol' jecky with a cargo worth fifty thousand times the price o' her new? Why, when it was comin' in, there was a hush like the king hisself was bein' buried."

Brand looked at the boyish Knight, the junior purser, twenty years old, and at Gopal Singh. Knight was grinning widely at all this talk, but Singh covered his feelings well. Perhaps years of seeing poverty had taught him that thoughts of gold were dangerous. He was a handsome fellow, tall and thin like Eric.

Knight chipped in, his young cheeks burning brightly, "I kept countin' as they came through, an' when it passed a million pounds, I said I wouldn't torture myself anymore. Who needs more than a million pounds?"

Chief Engineer Watts and Second Officer Nikolin,

both lime-sour, did not join in. But their ears were perked up, Brand noticed.

Yes, it was the same as it had always been, Brand reassured himself. It was a fever that miners first felt at Witwatersrand, in the Transvaal; and then, like a plague, it crept from the earth to the smelting of the gold; and then the fever followed the bullion bars as they were shaped. It was a fever centuries old. Incurable.

"Mueller died this afternoon," Captain Brand said to them all.

There was a momentary hush, and a few words about Mueller. Then talk of the bullion continued as if Mueller had never lived.

It was cleaner on the bridge. The sky over South Africa was shot through with stars. A light breeze plucked at the ship.

Fools, Brand said to himself as he upped his body into the high-backed swivel chair. But again, the gold was something to talk about. That was a most precious commodity at sea.

Brand turned his head westward, where the clear night exposed the hump of shore accentuated here and there by dim lights. He owed the Bank of South Africa nothing but a hard time, he thought. He was fifty-six years old and had the *Massinga* as his entire life's work, his only asset. For scrap, which she soon would be, maybe twenty thousand pounds. Less, probably. That was a lot of money, of course. But God knows, he'd fought for every bob of it.

Once, when Angela was alive, he'd dreamed of something called the Brand Lines. Solid name, that. Every master who owned a vessel, or shared in ownership, had dreams like that. In time, Eric would have been a first officer, then a captain in the Brand Lines. They were dreams that kept you from going crazy in endless waters; dreams that took the place of home, the hearth of love. You kept madness away by replacing it with floating empires. Then *they* floated away.

Brand swiveled around, looking down toward the specie room, tucked aft off Number 3 hatch. The gold almost pulsed in the night. How would one go about it on a ship like the *Massinga*? How would you do it, and be above suspicion? Three separate locks, each working individually, and three keys. To do it would require Calkins and Westmann, and they might not to be inclined to turn thief. And, of course, the bank would target them immediately; they would be hunted down and jailed.

I'm too old, Brand thought, *too bloody old to run for the next ten years*.

He laughed aloud. Until now, this chance trip, he'd never thought seriously about stealing anything more than a kiss. No, that wasn't at all true. During the twelve years when he'd cried out at night for fear of losing the *Massinga*, he'd thought about it occasionally. Face it—he'd hated the Bank of South Africa.

Just before midnight, Brand slipped off his chair again, strolled into the wheelhouse, exchanged a few words of no consequence with Gopal Singh, and then paused by the chart room to check the dead-reckoning course. They were piloting south, taking cuts on very familiar lights. Navigation this night was simple. The *Massinga* ran as if glued to invisible tracks.

Brand got into his bed, read for a half hour, and then turned out the light.

At about 2:00 A.M., Captain Brand sat up in bed, thinking: *You don't go into the specie room at all. You enter the mail room. You open the locker beside the port bulkhead, cut a hole in to reach the ventilating shaft. You crawl along the vent shaft to a position over the mail room, then you cut another hole. The welded door is never disturbed. Until Southampton, no one will know the gold is gone. By then, it will be long gone; transferred. Quite simple.*

Once this thought of theft was out, shaped, and polished a bit, Captain Brand turned on his side and went contentedly to sleep.

He awakened about seven and rang for his fifteen-year-old cabin boy, who always brought up sliced oranges, a bowl of brown-sugared porridge with rich cream, and coffee. Smiling, Brand said to Moosa, who'd been born dirt-poor on the banks of the Congo River, "Have you ever thought about stealing a lot of money?"

"No, sirrah. No, sirrah . . . ," the Bantu lad said, with a wide frown.

"I thought about it last night, and sometime before you die you'll think about it."

"Yes, sirrah. Yes, sirrah . . ." He looked frantically at the door.

"You may go," said Captain Brand.

Moosa fled from such talk.

Over breakfast in his cabin, Brand scanned Lowe's neat file of the night's news. In addition to being the radio operator, Sparks was something of an editor. The one-legged Welshman, a *Massinga* old-timer, was very smart, a thinker and a reader. He copied the wire briefs out of Jo'burg, boiling down the best of the news, occasionally adding a comment of his own.

This morning the radio operator had jotted, "Serves them right," on one paragraph.

Captain Brand studied it with a quizzical look. It was datelined Durban, an announcement from the Castle Lines. Their investigation of the *Kimberly Castle* had proved that sabotage had been accomplished on the engines. Brand read the paragraph twice. Infrequently, it happened. An oiler or wiper, angry at the chief, would foul up the engines; a seaman, suffering from low pay, might start a fire in the paint locker, getting his licks against the shipping company.

Brand's usual morning inspection began at the fo'c'sle head and went aft along the main deck, up over the after boat deck, then down to the stern. It was always a brisk business, for he knew the *Massinga* bilges to crosstrees. His riveting eyes could catch any sailor's sin, any defect, as Calkins had sadly learned. He circled the *Massinga*, port and starboard, in ten minutes and then went below decks, his steel-plated shoes knocking the hemp runners as he wound through the dim midships passages.

On the port side, opposite the mail room, he stopped a moment, gazing at the locker. It was seldom opened, being a storage space for supplemental handheld fire extinguishers. The locker was five feet high and about three deep. A sloppy sailor had painted over the key insert several months before, but now that white coat had been scratched to reveal brass.

Brand stared at it, held the torch on it for several seconds, scanned the deserted passageway, and then hurried up a pair of ladders to Calkins's office. Mohandas, the Lascar boy who was on duty, fell apart when Brand barged in, a cockle-sized whirlwind. Mohandas had been dozing.

Brand snapped, "Go aft for coffee."

The boy, wheezing out, "Sahib," fled with a look of fright on his face.

Brand's eyes swept Calkins's big keyboard from row to row until he found EXTINGUISHER LOCKER, PORT SIDE, MIDSHIPS. He nabbed the key off the hook and descended again to the third deck. He was breathing hard as he unsnapped the lock and drove the beam of the torch inside the sheet-steel box. Then he laughed harshly. Yes, five of the extinguishers had been removed and then replaced. The dust had been disturbed. Somebody had been examining the locker, without doubt.

Replacing the key, Brand located Mr. Calkins on the forward main deck and said, "Mr. Calkins, it is time for us to check the bullion. Please summon Westmann. I'll meet you outside the specie room door."

In a few minutes, they were gathered.

Brand said, "Gentlemen, this is a little ritual that we must go through each morning until we arrive at Southampton." He looked at Westmann. "We must see that no one has made off with the gold during the night."

Westmann laughed nervously. "Sooch a big vaste o' time."

"But necessary," Brand replied. "Insert your key, Mr. Westmann."

The fat Hollander nodded and opened the first lock.

"Mr. Calkins."

His key clicked. "All the way to Southampton?" Calkins muttered.

Brand nodded, then turned his key, breaking the heavy handle to the right almost simultaneously and pulling the door open. He reached inside to flick the switch. The room flooded with light and they all stared at the precise stacks of boxes, each with its seal facing the door. Calkins cleared his throat; Westmann murmured, *"Hmn . . ."*

Brand was amused at their reactions but glanced only at Westmann. He was the logical candidate, all right.

"Are you satisfied, gentlemen?" They grunted and nodded. He doused the light, swung the door shut, and they all proceeded to relock.

Brand held out a long sheet of paper, extracting a pen from his breast pocket. "Now, please sign the inspection sheet."

Calkins blinked.

"It simply states that we found the bullion in good order," Brand assured him.

"De mail rawm?" Westmann asked. "Vee cannot sign for de mail rawm."

"Of course not," Brand said. "We cannot see through a welded steel door. We presume the gold is safe in there. Just sign."

Back in his bridge chair, Captain Brand thoughtfully surveyed the sea. Now, who was it? Who was this second brilliant man aboard? Who had thought of the same idea to get at the bullion in the mail room? He ticked them all off, from Calkins down. He even included the old chief engineer, Watts. A cutting torch would be necessary. Westmann, the Dutchman, was the uppermost candidate. Yet, on second thought, he was lardy, almost as lardy as Calkins. Both too fat to squeeze down that venting system.

In the two remaining hours before noon, Brand punished his brain. Then suddenly it all fell in place. The sabotage on the *Kimberly Castle*, forcing the bank's use of the *Massinga*; Mueller's brutal beating in Durban, forcing substitution of a new mate, the young Indian from Mangalore, Gopal Singh; the excess bullion, forcing use of the mail room. It was a daring plan—clever as stealing the crown jewels, thought Brand—one that required close study of the *Massinga*'s construction; one that required outside help.

Brand swiveled around to look with wonder at the slimhipped, athletic Singh, who was standing innocently in the wheelhouse, gazing forward. He could go through those vent pipes like a speedy snake.

Brand grinned. "Well, I'll be double-damned. *I will be double-damned.*" The young man who reminded him of Eric was likely a thief.

Then he swiveled back to put his binoculars on a dhow that was beating north past them. It certainly wouldn't be that dhow. But another, crewed by scurvy no-accounts who'd happily kill for five pounds. It was a cinch that Singh had partners. But Singh—and whoever was behind him—would be lucky to get their bullion to Bombay.

Skipping lunch, Brand stayed on the bridge until they made anchorage at Port Elizabeth, thinking only of what was about to occur.

The *Massinga* had to load wheat, cotton, wool, hides, and a few bales of ostrich feathers at Port Elizabeth. For the first time within his memory, Brand was not interested in the noisy process of loading from the chunky wooden lighters. The small barges were tied to both sides of the *Massinga*.

Brand had a hunch that Singh would go ashore. Purpose: to make final arrangements for the dhow. And Brand had also selected Mossel Bay, his next port, as the off-take point for the bullion. Cape Town would be difficult; Las Palmas, impossible. Equally so, Southampton. No, Mr. Singh would undoubtedly try to accomplish the theft during the stay at Mossel Bay.

At 3:00 P.M., Brand watched as the athletic Indian jumped from a lighter deck into a water taxi. It sped toward Port Elizabeth's jetty, which seemed to be anchored beneath the quaint, skinny tower that dominated the city's profile.

When its wake was a mere white fuzz on the roadstead, Brand eased down to revisit Calkins's office. The first officer was on deck by Number 5 hatch, and once again Brand chased off the mystified Mohandas. This time, he selected Singh's extra key from the board and went straight to the Indian's cabin.

Brand tightened his nostrils as he entered the darkened cubicle. The cabin stank. The air inside was putrid with body smells. Brand opened the vertical clothes locker and poked around. Then he quickly checked the small writing-desk drawer, and finally turned his attention to the larger drawers beneath the bunk.

In the bottom drawer, under work clothes, he found what he was searching for—a new, very compact cutting torch, with two flasks. London-made, it was a simple but decisive instrument. One flask would be enough for the bulkhead behind the fire extinguisher locker; the other was sufficient for the mail room overhead, and for entry into Number 3 cargo hold.

There was even a tidy little breathing mask to counter the torch fumes within the vent space. Pass the bullion up, load it on a cargo pallet, cover it with burlap, and up and off it would go.

Brand nodded to himself and carefully spread the work clothes back over the cutter and mask, closed the drawer, and exited into the passageway. A clever, clever plan—obviously not the brainwork of Gopal Singh alone.

The day dwindled over Algoa Bay, and the light became thin and pale as the sun angled down behind the vast Drakensberg Range. Captain Brand waited thoughtfully on the bridge until he saw a water taxi bearing down on the *Massinga*. Leaning against the rail, he watched as Singh balanced on the prow of the boat, then jumped easily to the lighter deck, landing gracefully on his toes. *Singh could navigate that vent as if he lived in it*, Brand thought. Brand stretched and went below for dinner.

During the long afternoon, he'd thought about Lady Fate and how fickle the wraith was. Here he was, playing with the idea of Calkins and Westmann partnering him in some fancy theft, and he was summarily handed a stranger, Third Officer Gopal Ramji Singh, who was in earnest. It was much better. Singh could vanish behind Mangalore, into the Kolar, and no man of white skin would ever find him.

A stroke of unbelievable luck if Brand was willing to seize it. Half to Singh and whoever was backing him; half to Harry Brand. An enormously fair arrangement. One million pounds each. Retirement in the Seychelles after the *Massinga* was scrapped.

But how did one go about collecting, once the bullion was in the dhow and on its way? Trust the dhow captain? Ho, ho! That dhow business was a stumper. But there were always answers. Perhaps the best way was not to let the gold go in the dhow at all. Off-load in Las Palmas—he knew a quiet, safe warehouse—pick it up on the way back, then proceed to Bombay with Gopal Ramji Singh as, you might say, an amicable hostage. The main thing was the bullion's removal from the mail room.

And there was the question of Singh's partner. Could it be high-and-mighty, snooty Mr. Chapman, from the Bank of South Africa? Somebody had known about, or planned, well in advance that excess bullion that could not be handled in the specie room. Mr. Chapman himself, perhaps. *Oh, Mr. Chapman, do I have a surprise for you*, thought Captain Brand joyfully.

He had a leisurely dinner of roast lamb and mint sauce, boiled new potatoes and tiny fresh peas, and tapioca pudding, and then at about eight-thirty requested that Singh come to his cabin.

The Indian was most polite, even humble.

"Sit down, Mr. Singh," Brand said.

Singh nodded and took a seat, his black eyes a touch uneasy. Brand opened a teak box and proffered a long, thick Dutch-made cigar.

"I do not smoke, sir," said Singh.

Brand smiled, "Neither do I. Bad habit. Like drinking. But I have these for important guests."

Singh's eyes narrowed. "You consider me of importance?"

"Yes." Brand nodded. "Very much so, Mr. Singh. You are one of my officers."

Singh shifted on his chair. He suddenly seemed very uncomfortable.

"Was your trip ashore pleasant?" Brand asked.

"Very, sir," replied Singh.

Brand regarded Singh in silence for a long time. He thought about the bullion in the mail room and about the Bank of South Africa. He thought about his age and about retiring to the Seychelles, but he could not bring himself to make a proposition to this man. They'd killed Mueller. And he didn't like the idea of the *Massinga* going into a scrap yard with her name soiled by theft. It had been Angela's idea to buy her.

Singh interrupted his thoughts. "Why did you summon me here, sir?"

Brand replied stiffly, "I usually ask my new officers to see me here in private. I like to know them." He paused. "But since you don't smoke"—he paused again, feeling slightly ill—"you may go, Mr. Singh. We'll talk again at a later time."

Singh rose and nodded politely. He murmured, "Thank you for your hospitality, Captain," and left, a puzzled look on his dark face.

As the door closed, Brand thought of Angela and Eric, and suddenly he felt like vomiting. He staggered into the bathroom, stuck his finger down his throat, and did indeed vomit. Sweating profusely, he stood by the bowl and cursed the Bank of South Africa. It was a bloody monster, as big as the Drakensberg Range, as honest as the sea itself, as mean as the jags of a coral head. But dammit all, it commanded respect as well as hatred.

Harry Brand sighed. And the *Massinga* commanded respect, as did Brand himself. He might have been a drunk for a while but he was never a thief.

The ship was quiet the rest of the night. In his bed, Brand could hear the blowers humming and the fainter sounds of the auxiliaries working away in the engine room. He knew that Singh, off watch, was inside the locker, perhaps already in the vent crawl, using the superb torch to knife away the steel in a man-sized hole. A brave, gutsy man. Brand decided to let him take his head. Otherwise Mueller's killers would never be found. Otherwise the man who was manipulating Singh would never be identified.

Brand slept little until dawn.

Two days later, at Mossel Bay, a comparatively short distance from Port Elizabeth, Captain Brand was churlish at the 9:00 A.M. bullion inspection. Anxious to get it over with. Above and outside, Brand and his officers could hear the rumble of the winches, the slapping sounds of the slings and runners, the hubbub of loading and unloading. Calkins looked pale, not at all his hearty self, Brand noticed.

When the door was locked again and the sheet signed, Brand went to his cabin, opened his safe to return his key to the tin drawer, and withdrew a pistol. He checked the action of the .38 and loaded it. He hoped Singh would behave and reveal his partners; Brand couldn't help liking him, though he was a misguided scoundrel. Then he slipped the gun into his coat pocket and went to the port wing of the bridge, reaching there just as the wheelhouse phone rang.

It was Calkins. He sounded ill. "Cap'n, I've asked Singh to relieve me on deck. I must have eaten something bad."

Brand frowned. Was Calkins mixed up in it? Doubtful. Probably temporarily poisoned. They'd had curry the night before—an easy food to poison, the hot taste disguising almost any chemical.

Brand said, "All right, Mr. Calkins, rest easy. I'll keep an eye on things." He returned to the bridge wing.

Singh was already on deck, being very efficient. The booms on Number 3 hatch were rigged out. There was cargo, canned goods trans-shipped from Durban to Mossel Bay, in Number 3. An hour's work, two maybe.

Brand watched as the first lift came up from the hold, swaying gently, riding the pallet. Then it was winched out over the side and lowered to the deck of the lighter. It was an unusually small lighter, Brand noticed. That was puzzling, too.

Brand lifted his vision forward, a few points off the bow. A dhow was anchored about a hundred yards away. Its crew was going about its business with rare nonchalance. Brand watched Singh closely. He never so much as gave the dhow a glance. In fact, he ignored the dhow until the small lighter was chock-a-block.

Then Singh shouted up, "Sir, we cannot load any more on her. What about using the dhow?" He nodded toward the craft. "We only have one more pallet to go."

The bullion! Marveling at the gaudy nerve of the Indian, Brand nodded, and Singh shouted across to the dhow, speaking in fluent, rapid Tamil. Crewmen scurried to the bow to weigh anchor and come alongside. The diesel in the dhow rumbled.

Beneath the windscreen, Brand slipped the .38 from his pocket and held it loosely. Why, Singh was going to steal the gold right under his very nose, *as he watched*. The man had the nerve of a cobra.

Then Brand looked down on deck. Tufti, the big Kaffir winchman, was now taking up. The lifting cable put a heavy strain on the slings. The cable almost sang with weight. Tufti frowned, then went to the hatch to peer down. He shrugged and came back to the controls, adding more power. Brand knew it was the bullion from the mail room.

Slowly, the load emerged past the coamings of the hatch, a huge square boxed with two-by-sixes, bur-lapped beneath—identical to the other loads that had been coming out of Number 3. Identical except for weight.

Brand watched in mute fascination as the pallet reached midair position over Number 3, ready for Tufti's deft haul-out over the side. Then he barked to Tufti, "Hold up there. Stop it off."

The heavy pallet swayed.

Singh, his mouth open, was frozen. He stared up at the bridge toward Brand, his handsome face taut, his black eyes wide and stunned. Then he looked toward the dhow, which was sliding against the lighter.

Brand yelled, "Singh, you bloody gold thief!"

The Indian began to run for the chains.

Brand shouted, "Don't be a damn fool, man, stay where you are!"

But Singh didn't stop. Brand lifted the .38 and aimed, but didn't pull the trigger. He'd already killed one man for the Bank of South Africa. Brand fired the .38 into the air. Hearing the shot, Singh stopped, then dove into the water and swam rapidly away.

For a moment the dhow crew was in shock. Then a tall, bearded man on the stern barked orders, and long poles shoved her off from the lighter. Diesel smoke puffed from her side, and the dhow got under way.

Brand made no move as Calkins's Lascar boy, Mohandas, dove from the boat deck and swam for shore. *Oh, ho*, Brand thought, *Singh also had some inside help*. But Mohandas wasn't the main culprit. Brand still suspected Chapman.

For a moment now, the *Massinga* was paralyzed, and Captain Brand suddenly realized he'd started to quiver, something he had not done when he'd shot the Cockney, poor devil, in 1962. He felt sorry for Singh and his weakness. But he understood the lust.

Tufti called up, "Sar, what do we do wit dis load?"

Brand answered, "Stay by it, Tufti."

The Kaffir nodded and relaxed by his winch box.

Brand shouted down, "It's gold, Tufti."

The black man's flat face went skyward and he looked at the dangling square bundle. It hung in the blinding Mossel Bay sun like a severed lion's head. Tufti's tongue licked out, a normal reaction.

Brand looked at the mass suspended in the hot air. It was a terrible cargo. Brand wiped away the sweat around his eyes.

"Take the stopper off, Tufti," Brand called down to the winchman.

Tufti frowned, took the stopper off, then turned the handle on the winch box; the heavy pallet swung outboard. Brand held up his hand as soon as it cleared the ship. He looked over to the port wing and walked that way. The lighter was still in position, a dozen feet aft of the dangling load of bullion.

Suddenly Brand was aware that most of the men

on the *Massinga* were on the foredeck, looking at the dangling gold. The Kaffirs were there, the Chinese galley help, the Bantus, the Lascars, the London dock scum, Knight, Westmann, even Watts and Nikolin.

For a moment Brand rubbed the *Massinga*'s bridge rail lovingly. She'd never carry gold again, for certain, but that was all right. In a voice nearer soft than hard, he ordered, "Drop it, Tufti."

The Kaffir was stunned. In twenty years, he'd never dropped a load, accidentally or otherwise.

"Drop it," Brand repeated.

The cable sang and the pallet hit the water with a splash. Tufti dashed away, for the cable would soon rip off the drum and snake wildly about the deck.

But Brand was not looking at Tufti. He was watching the foam and bubbles on top of the water. He did hear the odd cheer that broke from the foredeck of the *Massinga*. Men lusted for bullion but hated it more than they realized.

He stayed on the bridge wing a moment longer, then proceeded to the radio shack. Sitting on the edge of Sparks's desk, he dictated: "BSA—Durban. Request you make immediate arrangements off-load all bullion from this vessel. Stop. Sorry inform you some mail room bullion now bottom of sea due accident off-loading. Stop. Have enjoyed my long relationship with BSA but believe best terminate. Stop. Suggest you check association between Mr. Chapman and my former third officer, Gopal Ramji Singh. Stop. Respectfully, H. Brand. Master M.V. *Massinga*."

Sparks blinked. "Was there a relationship between Chapman and Singh?"

Brand grinned. "I don't know. That's for the Bank of South Africa to find out!"

Looking and feeling quite chipper, he departed the radio shack. Angela and Eric would have been proud.

Wingman, Fly Me Down!

*T*here was a roar. A white flash. Then complete darkness. Cold wind hammered Lieutenant Grimes's face. Seconds later, a voice ebbed into the sickening spiral of semiconsciousness: "You're losing fuel from your right wing tank." It was Pete Lynn, Grimes's wingman, his flying partner.

Fuel? Wing tank? Are you crazy, Lynn? Grimes thought.

His hands began to grope in the cockpit. Then he realized something very strange—he was blind.

He felt for his lip mike and found it behind his crash helmet. His oxygen mask had been torn away. Swallowing hard to clear his throat of blood, he answered, "I can't see." And death, he knew, was sitting beside him on this September morning, 1950.

During the next thirty minutes, over North Korea and the Yellow Sea, his life was in the hands of Wingman Lynn.

A little earlier, Grimes and Lynn, also a lieutenant, junior grade, had lingered sleepily in the wardroom of the aircraft carrier *Philippine Sea*. Then they went up to the ready room to tog out in flight gear. Lynn was Grimes's regular wingman—usually flying about a hundred yards astern and out to the right forty-five degrees. They'd racked up nine combat missions in the Korean War together and were both happy with the arrangement. For a pair of combat novices they felt pretty rugged. In their own opinion, they were "hot" pilots, very much capable of combat with the enemy.

Tom Shanahan, the briefing officer, called for quiet in the ready room. After a general rundown, he repeated their specific mission: "Grimes and Lynn, go up and take a look at the Pyong-gang airfield. Then follow the railroad back to Seoul." Seoul, the capital of South Korea, had been occupied by North Korean troops in July.

The communist North Koreans had invaded South Korea on June 25, 1950, and the United States had responded almost immediately with ships of the Seventh Fleet. The *Philippine Sea*, flagship of Task Group Yoke, operated with Task Force 77, the navy's seaborne strike force. She'd been on station since early August.

The Pyong-gang strip, a pesky secondary landing strip, had been irritating to the navy. Shanahan explained it was grass and looked like any farmer's field.

Lynn frowned, saying, "He's described the needle. Now all we have to do is find it in the haystack." Shanahan instructed them to strafe any enemy planes caught on the ground. They had guns and rockets to do the job.

"Any questions?" Shanahan asked.

There were none. When the ready room squawk

blared, "Pilots, man your planes," they double-timed up to the flight deck.

Grimes took a turn around his plane—a Grumman Panther F$_9$F fighter with a Pratt & Whitney turbo-jet engine—checking the wheels, flaps, wings, and tail. The plane was noted for its short takeoff run and low landing speed. Lynn made the same routine inspection of his Panther.

The *Philippine Sea* was steady, moving swiftly over the water's smooth surface off the west coast of Korea. *Nice day for flying*, Grimes thought. The sun was warm, shining brightly.

After rubbing his good-luck piece, a Chinese dollar, he climbed aboard the Panther, with the white 216 on her fuselage. He started her up and checked out the instruments. She trembled a little bit as he slowly opened power, then she began to thunder without complaint. He eased her off and taxied to the starboard catapult. After the launch crew tied him down, he released his brakes and ran her up again. All OK.

The catapult officer was poking two fingers in the air. *Off you go!* Grimes gave her full power and saluted the "cat" officer with a "let her rip" signal. *Whoomp!* From zero to ninety miles an hour in ninety feet.

He was airborne and gaining altitude. It was 0734 and he slowed until Lynn, who was next up for the "cat shot," joined him.

Turning east, they leveled out at fifteen thousand feet for the ride in. There was hardly a ripple on the Yellow Sea. A few wispy clouds were drifting high and inshore. A real champagne day for flying.

Grimes settled back, after waving a welcome to Lynn, and flew the Panther easily. She had thirty-

eight feet of wings and he could get 550 knots out
of her in level flight. For now, she hummed along
at 370 knots without a strain. He began singing as
they neared the coast. There was not much to do in
the cockpit except sight-see on a straightaway.

Motioning down, he called Lynn. "How's that?"
he shouted.

Reflection from the sun was laying a coat of gold
over the water around the American and British invasion ships in Inchon Harbor. They looked like
chips of wood in a big blue bathtub. Except for the
oily smoke around Inchon, it could have been a re-
gatta day.

They cleared the coast and started for Pyong-gang,
skirting by Seoul and passing Kaesong to the east.
The mountains were still summer green. Some of
them were terraced—gently stair-stepped down the
sides.

With Lynn close behind, Grimes turned the Panther's nose and leveled at four thousand feet as they
neared Pyong-gang. They plodded right into that
measly airfield like a pair of bird dogs on a holiday.
It was as lively as a tomb. A few Russian-type aircraft, burned and shattered, dotted the grassy run-
ways. No flyable enemy aircraft.

Grimes flagged Lynn. "Nothing here. Let's go to
Seoul."

A dinky railroad, with a track about five feet wide,
wound around the valley to Seoul. They wheeled
around in the peaceful sky and dropped low to follow the toy tracks. It was mountainous on either
side, with varying heights up to a thousand feet.

Halfway there Grimes spotted a locomotive
stopped on the tracks. He yelled to Lynn, "Got us
a choo-choo."

The wingman pulled in behind Grimes, who opened up when the engine came in range. Grimes saw his wing gun tracers slam into the boiler. The engine began to burn, and Lynn gave it a departing dose.

They swung around the outskirts of Seoul and had a welcome party waiting at about four thousand feet. Antiaircraft fire! Puffs and concussions were growing closer. The ack-ack fire buffeted the Panthers about and the pilots climbed higher.

Grimes looked back to see how Lynn was doing. The wingman yelled, "Ya-hoo!" and they exchanged grins.

They started northwest on the leg up the Han River, headed back for the ship, disappointed at the lack of targets. One old, beaten-up locomotive wasn't worth the fuel and ammunition expended. Then Grimes spotted a string of motor sampans crossing the river. Maybe a chance to score higher.

"Let's look them over," he said, and they dove to about two hundred feet. The engines whined nicely on both aircraft. The sampans were crossing in lines. He estimated seventy-five boats and held fire to see if they were refugees.

Troops! Grimes and Lynn began firing. Grimes could see the soldiers jumping out of the boats. Twenty-millimeter guns were built for work like this. The sampans began to burn and sink.

Lynn, in a tight wing position, was mopping up to the right, seventy-five yards astern.

Just before Grimes reached the last line of sampans, he glanced toward the south shore. A sampan was shoving off. A soldier jumped out and knelt. It appeared he had a rifle. He wasn't worth bothering with and Grimes looked forward again.

Something dead ahead. He caught a whisker of it. *Then the roar and the flash.* He'd been sucked into the oldest known military weapon—a mantrap. Three steel cables had been stretched across the river to bring down aircraft. He'd snapped them like twine.

Everything was black. Biting wind rushed over him. For an instant Grimes didn't know where he was, what he was doing. Then he heard the Pratt & Whitney boiling along. The slant of his body told him that the Panther was climbing steeply.

Lynn repeated: "You're losing fuel . . ."

Grimes's hands and arms felt OK. He tried to wipe his eyes out. It got hazily light. Then even the light faded away. The wind was hitting him like a fist, so he knew he'd lost the cockpit canopy. With one hand he gripped the stick but didn't alter the setting. On every low sweep he always had plenty of back trim on the elevators. The plane would automatically climb if anything happened. The old fighter-pilot trick paid off.

"What's wrong?" Lynn asked.

"I'm blind!"

"You're blind?" Lynn repeated, in a hollow voice, as if that condition were impossible. *Pilots can't be blind.*

"I can't see, Pete!"

There was a moment of stunned silence from Lynn.

"Tell me how to fly this thing," Grimes pleaded.

"OK, I'm going to level you out at two thousand."

Grimes felt relief knowing that he was a safe distance off the ground. Lynn coached him up another five hundred feet. "Little more, Jack. Little more."

Then, "Hold it."

"Now come left," Lynn said. How far left? Eyesight is such a precious thing, even walking across a room. Flying an airplane, it goes far beyond, becoming critical.

In the howling darkness, he came left and waited until Lynn said, "Steady now."

He tried to spit out the blood that was in his throat but the wind kept it in his mouth. He swallowed it.

The wind seemed to be pushing from all angles, and he definitely knew that the canopy was gone. He also knew that the side panels of his windshield had splintered away in a hail of glass.

"Jack, I'm going to come alongside you . . ."

He didn't try to turn his head. It hurt with each movement. He could feel the tear in his cheek opening wider as the wind pocketed, so he shut his lips as much as he could.

"I got to slow down," he said, easing the throttle in. His whole face threatened to open up.

"Don't stall her," Lynn said.

Grimes laughed at that. Why, he didn't know. But the pain from the laugh shot up into his head.

He could hear Lynn's plane alongside him, flying dangerously close to a blind man who could at any split second pass out or panic.

Then Lynn's voice broke in again: "Jack, your right wingtip is shattered. Nose of your plane split halfway to the cockpit. Your canopy is busted . . ."

Grimes thought he'd never stop. In one way, it was lousy psychology. But Lynn thought that Grimes should know what his problems were—or most of them. In fact, there was one problem he left off his list. Grimes's right wing had been partially ripped away at the root. There was a possibility that it would shear off. Lynn decided Grimes had enough to worry about without knowing that.

"Keep her steady," said Lynn, in an encouraging voice.

Grimes could picture him out to the side, pacing along, a broad jump away.

"Can you fly wing on *me?*" Lynn asked.

"For God's sake, Pete, I'm blind."

"I know. There's a red haze all around your cockpit. I can't even see you clearly."

The blood was spraying out in a fine mist from Grimes's wounds.

"I'll keep flying wing on *you*," Lynn said.

For the next few minutes, Lynn nursed him along, telling him to come left or right; pull up a bit.

Grimes's hands were beginning to get heavy. His feet were leaden. He was slipping in and out of shock.

Lynn spoke again: "How about trying Kimpo?"

Grimes didn't answer but heard Lynn calling the command ship at Inchon, the invasion site. "Do we have Kimpo yet?" Lynn repeated it again and again.

Then the answer came back from the USS *Mt. McKinley*. It was a sympathetic negative. The Marines were fighting for Kimpo at that moment. The *McKinley* advised a crash landing near the ships in the harbor.

Tides were extreme at Inchon. There was a low, wide belt of mud at low water. Grimes would hit that ooze if he missed the water and knew it. He'd seen one pilot pancake into mud and suffocate.

Although he was getting weaker by the minute, he said, "Let's go to the ship."

"OK, Jack, I'm taking you home. Ease to your right."

Grimes thought he could get home providing he did his part. He trusted Lynn. He knew it would be his fault if he went chicken in trying to land blind.

Lynn came in again. "How about fuel?"

Fuel? Depending on speed and altitude, the Panther can fly from ninety minutes to three hours. But he'd lost his reserve from the wing tank and couldn't see the gauge. He'd been up almost two hours. He began to pray. God willing, that turbo-jet would keep on whining.

"Carrier!" Lynn shouted suddenly. He turned Grimes north and straightened him out.

"You're doing fine, boy," Lynn said soothingly.

Despite the stinging cold, Grimes's body was hot with sweat. His heart was pounding. Landing on a flattop with all your faculties is difficult enough. Sitting down on it without seeing it is almost unthinkable.

"Jack, she's British," said Lynn, in a tight voice.

Grimes saw his chances skittering away. Sure, if he had to he'd try to land on a strange ship. But all carrier pilots knew their own ships best, their own crews best. Maybe the British could land him safely, maybe not. Just one wrong move and he could plow into the stern of the ship or hit the bridge.

Then faintly he heard another voice. "Magnetic heading to ship is two-three-zero." He recognized Phil Stanwood, his squadron leader. Stanwood had heard the cross-talk with Lynn. But he seemed far away. Lynn brought Grimes around to two-three-zero.

At almost the same moment, Grimes felt himself slipping away. The wind didn't seem so harsh. The blood draining from his face gave him a good tired feeling. He tried to stop the flow of the blood, reaching into his coverall for a bandage.

"Add power, Jack! Pull up! Pull up!" Lynn screamed. "You're going down."

The words were like a slap. Grimes added power and pulled the nose up.

Then he lay back again and tried to follow directions. He thought about his wife, Anne, at home in Memphis. She was seven months pregnant. *Hell of a thing*, he thought. *A baby but no father*. There was a small picture of Anne in his wallet, and he wanted to see it, perhaps for the last time. This was the worst moment of the entire half hour.

"Pull up. Pull!" Lynn screamed again.

Grimes was angry at his wingman for a few seconds but it didn't last long.

He felt like he was in a warm fog. Very lonely. He didn't care anymore. There was no pain now; no feeling. It seemed he'd been drifting along for hours. The engine roared steadily. The ride was gentle.

Another voice sliced in: "Keep talking to him, Pete."

The voice belonged to Johnny White, the division leader.

Grimes perked up again, shaking his head to ward off sleep. He thought, *The whole U.S. Navy must be standing by to get me out of the air.* He began to fight the weakness, the drifting off. He knew he was getting near home.

Home was a strip of deck 83 feet wide and 880 feet long. He heard Lynn say, "Jack, I'm taking you into the downwind leg. Listen carefully . . ."

Lynn began to guide him in.

Grimes knew he had one approach to make. One

pass. One chance to stay alive and see Anne again, see the baby. He'd quit if the fuel didn't.

Lynn said calmly, "You're doing fine, old buddy." Then, "Put your wheels and tailhook down."

The navy puts blindfolds on its pilots and makes them locate every control and every instrument before checking out an aircraft. Grimes was humbly grateful at this moment for those high standards. He was flying by reflex now.

Then he heard Vance Lord, the landing signal officer. Under normal circumstances carrier pilots were wagged to the deck with hand signals. This was going to be a talk-down. Lynn had brought him home; now Lord was going to open the door.

"This is the LSO. Don't answer. Just listen. Take it easy," Lord said.

A moment passed.

"Too fast."

Grimes cut his speed.

"You're angling in too steep. Roll it out a bit."

Grimes complied. Vance, in spirit, was up there with him. The thought of Vance Lord giving him a wrong signal never entered his mind.

"You're in the slot now."

Grimes didn't have much strength left.

"High and to the right."

He fought her down and to the left.

Then there was absolute silence. Grimes could no longer hear the LSO's voice. He thought he'd passed over the ship.

"Cut it!" yelled Lord.

Grimes dropped the Panther's nose for a second, then pulled back on the stick to flare the landing. He felt the arresting hook grab. The Panther bounced and stopped.

Made it.

Someone wiped the blood from his eyes and he saw light through a red haze. Beautiful. He was lifted out of the cockpit. Then he tried to pull some heroics.

"I can walk," he said. He collapsed before he took a step.

In Sick Bay, Doc Chambers, the *Phil Sea*'s flight surgeon, made thirty-six stitches and put back some blood. He assessed the damage: nose split from the bridge to the end; both eyebrows laid open; left cheek torn back to the ear.

Several hours later, Grimes awakened to find Lynn by his side. "Gave me a real scare, boy."

Then other pilots came in to ask how he was. "Fine," he said.

In time, they cautiously asked how it felt to be up there blinded. He told them how a grown man can feel like a helpless child. Weak, scared, lonely.

He wrote Anne the next day and bragged a little about being the first pilot in history to make a blind carrier landing in a jet aircraft. He had trouble telling her how he felt about Pete Lynn and Vance Lord.

Later, he thought he should have told her that you can be a hot pilot but you can't live up there alone. *There's no such thing in carrier flying as a one-man show*, he should have told her. *You have to place your trust and your life in the calm voices and actions of the Lynns and Lords.*

He found that out in the half hour that death sat beside him in Panther 216.

Out There

Not five minutes after I cleared the Dana Harbor jetty in the *Spanker*, a sixteen-foot Boston Whaler, dense fog rolled in and I cut the Mercury 50 outboard to almost steerage way, two knots, groping along. Thick, wet mist takes away your sight but sharpens your hearing, fine-tunes your nerves.

Visibility was no more than twenty or thirty feet, and I crept south for about a quarter mile toward the red buoy that marked the harbor channel. I had planned to drift-fish about two miles offshore, let the boat ride the current and drag the bait along the bottom; if I had been lucky I would have caught a nice halibut or a big sand bass. But it was too risky out there in the fog. A large boat might have run me down accidentally. Instead I decided to drop anchor and fish by the buoy until the fog lifted. Sometimes in shallow water—if you didn't get tangled in kelp—croakers or calicos, sand bass will bite.

Before launching the boat I'd gone to Dana Wharf Sportsfishing for a plastic bag of frozen anchovies and another of squid. My dad always bought a half scoop of live bait but I couldn't afford the fifteen dollars the bait barge charged. Now I cut an anchovy in half and hooked the tail end, tossing the bait and sinker into the water, which I knew was about twelve feet deep in this spot. I'd fished these waters since I was a kid, mostly with a school friend, Buck Crowder, or my father. I settled back and opened a thermos of hot chocolate. My watch said the time was 6:40 A.M.

The foghorn on the jetty was bleating, and in the distance, more than a mile away on shore, the air horn on the San Diego-Los Angeles train kept breaking the early-morning peace.

I waited for almost another hour in the ghostly silence, small fish or perhaps crabs tapping the bait or stealing it. Then the fog began to slowly withdraw toward the west, leaving patches. A big cruiser, probably with radar, twin diesels boiling, passed not far away, barely visible; and the wake rocked the *Spanker*, tossing me back and forth on the stern seat.

In the middle of a toss, something, *something*, in the water toward shore startled me. I'm sure my mouth opened, and I know my heart drummed, for the *something* looked like a huge gray-green eel slowly moving on the gray surface, its blunt but serpentlike head awash, dark eyes the size of salad plates. Whatever it was, it must have measured twenty feet because, in my judgment, it was longer than the *Spanker*. I couldn't believe what I was seeing.

Barely breathing, I watched it disappear into a patch of low-lying fog. Only then did I realize I'd had a strike and the reel was screaming. Watching for the *thing* to reappear, I halfheartedly jerked back on the rod, hooking whatever had struck, not even bothering to heave in. For a moment, I wondered if I'd seen something that really wasn't there. Then I decided that I hadn't just imagined it. I'd seen a huge eel, or something that resembled an eel. It hadn't had fins or flippers, so it wasn't a fish or a whale. I held the twitching rod as if in a trance, more amazed than afraid.

I kept looking toward where the *thing* seemed to have disappeared, and then my attention was drawn to the other side. Coming out of the fog was a boat headed straight for the *Spanker*, but seemingly without power; adrift. A derelict, a sea ghost.

Jamming the rod butt beneath the seat, I began yelling, thinking that the owner of the boat was asleep or down below. It was a small white cabin cruiser. On it slowly came, and in a moment it bumped the *Spanker* on the port side. Scrambling to grab it by the bow chain, I kept yelling for the owner.

No answer, and I tied off to *Spanker*. Boat owners had no business sleeping while under way, powered or not.

Still no answer, and I decided to board the *Lotta Fun*, suddenly worried about what I might find. What else could happen this foggy morning? Was the owner just asleep, or had something else happened? I stepped aboard, noticing what I thought might be blood on the railing at the stern of the boat. It had a sheen and didn't look dried. Was it just fish blood or was it human blood? There was a small pool of it.

Cautiously I ducked into the tiny cabin, again asking for someone to respond. No one was home but I noticed a red light on the battery-powered coffee-pot and felt it. Hot! So someone had been aboard within the last few hours. I unhooked the pot and became aware of a smell in the boat that I hadn't noticed on boarding, a burnt-rubber odor.

I looked closer around the cabin and the interior deck but didn't see any more blood or any signs of a fight. On the counter near the small galley stove was an old battered tin lunch box. Someone had been getting ready to eat. Except for what was at the stern, it all looked normal.

Between sighting the huge eel and getting bumped by the derelict with the fresh blood on it, a core of fright was now lodged in my belly. I quickly re-boarded the *Spanker* and noticed the rod tip still bobbing. Trying to think of what to do next, I dislodged the rod butt from beneath the seat and reeled in. A small blue shark, tail whipping, came out of the water. I popped it loose.

Tow the *Lotta Fun* in and turn it over to Harbor Patrol, I finally decided. I led the boat around to my stern, flipped a line over its port bow cleat, and made it fast, then let out ten feet or so, just enough to control an easy haul. The sea was still calm, the fog still patchy.

I got under way, thinking that maybe there was some kind of connection between that giant eel, or whatever it was, and whoever had been aboard the *Lotta Fun*.

Dana Harbor Patrol is in a two-story building on a narrow island at the head of twin channels that are waterways leading to hundreds of boat berths, home to million-dollar yachts as well as humbler boats, fifteen-foot sailing types. The *Spanker* had a berth at the north end.

Harbor Patrol is a function of the Orange County Sheriff-Coroner Department. Fish and Game also operate out of the sheriff spaces. In back of the building are spaces for the patrol and rescue craft. Coming back through the jetties, where pelicans and gulls perch on gigantic rocks, I steered to the county berthing area, rehearsing what I was going to say.

I brought the *Lotta Fun* alongside the *Spanker*, then maneuvered both boats into an empty stall, jumped out on the dock, and tied them off fore and aft on cleats.

In a moment I was climbing the steps to the second-story patrol office and at the desk told the brown-uniformed duty sergeant that I'd just brought a drifting boat in; no one on it. "I tied it up at your dock. Name is *Lotta Fun*." Let them find the blood themselves.

I turned to leave, but Sergeant Lamont, who looked like he was midforties, a big man with a graying mustache, said, "Whoa! Let me get a report." He walked back to his desk, then returned to the counter with a form.

"OK, name, age, address . . ."

"Danny Aldo. I live at Seventy-two Trumpeter Way, Laguna Beach. I'm seventeen."

The sergeant wrote slowly, frowning. "You by yourself out there?"

"Yes, sir."

"Isn't seventeen a little young to be alone out in the ocean, even in clear weather? Your parents know?"

"My dad does. He owns the boat." He always says it's really "our" boat.

Lamont nodded. "Name of your boat and number?"

"*Spanker*. Sixteen-foot Boston Whaler." I dug out my wallet. "Charley-Fox, three-nine-zero-five, Jake-Zebra . . ."

"OK, what were you doing out there, and where were you?"

"I was fishing near the red buoy, had the anchor down, waiting for the fog to lift."

"And the *Lotta Fun* bumped into you?"

"Yes, sir, with no warning."

"What time?"

"About a half hour ago."

"You hear any voices, anyone calling for help before it hit you?"

"No, sir."

"You see anyone in the water?"

"No, sir."

"Anything at all unusual before it hit you?"

I hesitated, wondering whether or not I should tell Sergeant Lamont about the huge eel I saw just before the *Lotta Fun* showed up. Fish stories often made people laugh. But this was true and might have something to do with the *Lotta Fun* and its owner.

I took a deep breath and said, "Just before it bumped me, I saw a big green-gray eel come by about fifty feet away. It was longer than the *Spanker* and bigger around than a telephone pole."

Lamont's eyes rolled back in his head. "An eel longer than sixteen feet, bigger than a phone pole?"

"Yes, sir."

He made a face. "You sure you saw that?"

"Yes, sir."

"OK, I'll write it all down. And you were alone on your boat? The sixteen-foot eel comes by, then the *Lotta Fun* shows up, owner missing. I'm sure gonna get a call from Santa Ana on this one. Loch Ness Monster off Dana Point?''

I remained silent, thinking I shouldn't have told him about the eel.

''Anything else?''

I hesitated again. ''One more thing. When you go down to look at the *Lotta Fun* you'll see what I think is blood on the stern railing, portside. I don't know whether it's fish blood or human blood.''

''Whoops,'' said Sergeant Lamont. ''Why don't you just take a seat over there on that bench? I'll be back in a moment. I have to call investigators.''

I sat down on the bench, now wishing I'd heaved up my anchor, started the Mercury, and left all the trouble behind when I'd first seen the *Lotta Fun* coming. But my father had always taught me to render help to anyone who needed it at sea.

I had the feeling that my fishing day might be over.

About an hour later, the men from Santa Ana showed up. They read the sergeant's report, then approached me.

''Danny, I'm Deputy Roper, Orange County Sheriff's Department, and this is Deputy Cooper. Sergeant Lamont asked us to come down here and talk to you about that boat you brought in with the blood on it. Don't be frightened. Just relax. You're not being charged with anything.''

I was finding it hard to relax. ''Yes, sir.''

''Where is your father today?''

''In Washington, D.C., on business. He's a lawyer. I live with him. My mother lives in Denver. They're divorced.''

"And he approves of you going out alone? That's the truth?"

"Yes, sir. I'm a good sailor." My dad first took me fishing when I was three or four. These days, I always handle the boat when we go out.

"I bet you're a good sailor. Mind if I tape this interview?"

"No, sir."

Deputy Cooper said, "First things first. Sergeant Lamont has written here that you saw something unusual in the water before the *Lotta Fun* came along."

"A huge eel of some kind, I think. One eighteen or twenty feet long. It was this big around." I made an oval of my arms.

Cooper said, "Pardon me for laughing, but seals are never eighteen or twenty feet long."

"It wasn't a seal, sir. I've seen plenty of seals—there's a bell buoy about four miles north and they sleep and bark on top of it all the time. What I saw wasn't a seal. It wasn't a fish, either. It didn't have fins. It was longer than our boat. I think it was an eel."

Cooper shook his head, laughing again. "You sure you didn't have a bad dream out there, Danny? Like a sea serpent dream?" I disliked him immediately.

"I wasn't dreaming. I saw it."

"You expect us to believe you saw a sea monster? Well, I have to tell you, Danny boy, they don't exist."

"I didn't say I saw a sea monster, sir. Not a sea monster. It looked to me like a huge eel." I was sweating.

Roper sighed and said, "As a matter of fact, Phil, no one knows. Like UFOs, no one knows. But that's not what we're here to talk about. Let's get to the subject—that abandoned boat . . ."

Cooper asked, "OK, Danny, why didn't you radio in to Harbor Patrol and ask them to come out and check before you towed it in?"

"My dad put the radio on the boat just for me. But it's out of whack."

"You shouldn't have gone aboard, Danny," Cooper said. "If a crime has been committed, you contaminated the crime scene. Shoeprints, fingerprints—how do you know someone wasn't murdered?"

"I didn't even think about that, sir." Yes, I did. The blood!

"Our crime lab people are down there right now, and they'll make tests," Deputy Roper said. He added, "Sergeant Lamont checked the boat registration number with the Coast Guard. The *Lotta Fun* belongs to Jack Stokes, who lives here in Dana Point. Old guy, seventy-four. We've got people, including the local police, looking for him." Roper was the younger of the two. The nicer, too. Both wore civilian clothes.

"Do you think that big eel, or whatever it was, had anything to do with what happened on the *Lotta Fun?*" I asked.

"I doubt that very much," Roper replied.

"But the boat did drift up not long after I spotted whatever it was. Could that thing have knocked Mr. Stokes overboard, then swum up beside me?"

"Not likely," Roper answered.

"Pardon me for laughing again," Cooper said. "If Stokes fell overboard, it wasn't because of any sea monster."

I looked over at him. I hadn't said it was a sea monster.

"How do you account for the blood, Phil?" Roper asked.

"Fishermen cut themselves all the time. He cut himself, fainted, and fell overboard. No sea monster stuck its head up and grabbed old Jack . . ."

Buck Crowder called me the next morning about eight. "Hey, Danny, you made the *Times*. And they mentioned you on channel nine."

"I know." I had read the *Times* story quoting seventeen-year-old Danny Aldo as saying that the "sea monster" and the missing senior citizen might be somehow connected. It also quoted Deputy Phil Cooper as saying, "That kid gets A-plus for imagination. Sea monsters don't exist. Jack Stokes is the problem here."

The *Times* said that inquiries at Dana Wharf Sportsfishing had drawn laughter. "Sea monsters come out of bourbon bottles," one veteran fisherman said. "That boy ought to have his eyes examined," another said.

"I swear, Buck, I saw that thing, whatever it was."

"Yeah, but 'sea monster'?"

"Buck, I never did call it a sea monster. I keep saying that. Nobody listens. All I said was 'a big eel.' I don't even want to talk about it anymore."

"You're telling the truth?"

"I swear it."

"Damn, I wish I'd been out there with you. Man, I missed somethin'. That lousy dentist appointment."

We usually had fun. Fishing, laughing, talking. We both worked nights at Cones, the ice-cream and yogurt place fronting the inner harbor.

"Well, an eel twenty feet long, Danny. That's a very big eel," Buck said.

Yes, it was a very big eel.

"I faxed the *Times* story to my dad in Washington. He called me about an hour ago and laughed, then asked, 'Did it really happen that way?' I said it did. He said, 'I believe you; shame I wasn't there to be your witness. Keep me posted about Jack Stokes.' Maybe only my dad believes me."

Buck said, "OK, I believe you." But his voice was hollow.

"Yeah, you do . . ."

I took the Jeep and went for an In-and-Out hamburger, using phone order, then drove home again. On the drive back and forth, I got what I thought was a bright idea—use my dad's PC. As I ate, I logged onto our on-line service, and checked to see what their reference sources had on sea serpents/sea monsters/giant eels.

Up came:

In Greek mythology, Perseus, the son of Zeus and Danäe, encountered Andromeda, whom he saved from a fearful sea monster . . .

There were a half dozen other entries on sightings dated back to A.D. 300 and of no use whatsoever. It was all treated as mythology, anyway.

So I went on to the Internet, accessing the Library of Congress. Here I found more what I was looking for.

Just after noon, October 19, 1898, the sixty-five-foot wooden trawler *Eva Maria* was about eighty-five miles off Cape Blanco, Oregon, when the master, Alfonso Pombal, sighted something in the water off his starboard bow. It was swimming on the surface and he estimated it to be seventy or eighty feet long. With binoculars he determined it was not a whale. He called sleeping crewmen to the wheelhouse. The head was estimated to be at least twelve feet long. Pombal and his crewmen agreed it was some type of giant snake.

"I'm convinced we saw a sea serpent," said Captain Rober Faircloth, of the pollock fisher *Savoonga*, off the Aleutians in remarkably calm weather. A crewman mending a net saw a serpentlike creature at least twenty-five feet in length. He called Faircloth and soon the other crewmen joined them as witnesses. The creature kept pace with the *Savoonga* for at least three miles and seemed to be watching the boat. Incident was reported to the Coast Guard upon arrival at Dutch Harbor, June 23, 1926.

There were dozens of other cases, in both the Atlantic and the Pacific, as well as in foreign seas. One report said there'd been "thousands of such incidents," dating back to sailing-ship days. It was estimated that many other sightings were not reported by sailors because of fear of being laughed at. I could sympathize. The latest incident, one that caused me to slam the desk in triumph, had occurred not long ago. August 3, 1991: Having departed San Francisco en route to Los Angeles and Acapulco, the cruise liner *Pacific Empress* was about twenty miles off Point Concepcion, off the California coast, when:

> Captain Thomas Judy said, "I couldn't believe
> what I was seeing after the third mate called
> me to the bridge. I'd been at sea forty-five
> years, thirty-one as a master, and here was this
> huge sea-snake, maybe thirty feet long, off the
> port side, moving as fast as we were. The third
> mate ran to get his camera but by the time he
> was back on the bridge, the monster had dis-
> appeared. I can tell you it wasn't a whale, or a
> seal or a giant squid. It was a sea serpent,
> something I'd sworn never existed.

Point Concepcion wasn't all that far north of Dana
Point.

I called Buck to come by and take a look at what
the printer had spewed out. Buck read it and said,
"You weren't imagining things after all."

"Nope, I wasn't."

"Now, look at this one from the National Ocean-
ographic Data Center, Washington, D.C., 1989."

> Although we discount the fabled sea monsters,
> such as the kraken which could swallow ves-
> sels whole, we have not yet explored the ocean
> thoroughly enough to say with absolute cer-
> tainty that there are no monsters in the deep.
> Scientific observations and records note that gi-
> ant squid with tentacles forty feet long live at
> 1500 feet and that sizable objects have been
> detected by echo sounding at even greater
> depths. Oarfish 40 to 50 feet long have been
> observed by scientists. In recent years, Danish

scientists have studied large eel larvae that will grow to 90 feet if their growth rate is the same as other eel species.''

A day later I got a call from a Captain Patrick Carroll, who owned the swordfisher *Time of Joy*. I had watched her going out or coming in, sometimes flying the catch flag that meant she'd nailed one. I knew she tied up in front of Proud Mary's at the wharf. Carroll said he wanted to talk about what I'd seen, so I stopped by on my way to work.

The *Time of Joy* was about thirty feet in length, with a beam of nine or ten feet. She had a "pulpit," a harpooning platform that was drawn up while in harbor, and a crow's nest to look for swordfish.

I thought Carroll was about fifty, but no grizzled old seadog that you might find at the wharf bar in late afternoon. Though deep-tanned, he looked more like an insurance agent than a swordfisher. I had heard he'd been a college professor but discovered fishing was more fun than teaching.

Carroll said, "Have a seat." We were on the afterdeck. "Want coffee, Coke?"

"Coke'll be fine," I said, sitting on top of the engine box.

Carroll went into his combination wheelhouse, cookhouse, and bunkhouse and came back with two frosty cans. He put his bottom against the rail and said, "Get used to being called a liar. Long after they've found and forgotten Jack Stokes somebody around here will remember Danny Aldo and his sea monster. But I believe you. Sixteen years ago I saw something out there bigger than what you saw. Ever since, they've laughed about Pat Carroll and his sea monster. But I saw it . . .''

I frowned. Imagine being called a liar for sixteen years, almost the whole time I'd been on earth.

"Not only did I see it but I photographed it."

"And they still called you a liar."

He laughed and nodded. "Forty feet was my guess, and it looked like what you described to the sheriff's department."

"But how can we ever prove it?" I asked.

"Most scientists scoff at reports of strange giant sea creatures. They say 'Prove it,' and I say, 'Look at the *National Geographic* photos of fish at six thousand feet with big fanged heads and luminous eyes. No one can name the species. Plant life ceases to grow at six hundred feet and what's below, in darkness, is basically unknown. So-called sea monsters have washed ashore and scientists are embarrassed, calling them 'unknown species.'

"I've taken pictures. Even so, the first reaction is that you somehow faked the picture. People claimed I made a clay model, photographed it, then rephotographed it against water. Soon they've made a laughingstock out of you. Now I have a raft to throw overboard just for scale."

"You believe in sea monsters?"

Carroll shook his head. "I believe there are creatures that only a few people have seen. The oceans and seas are the most mysterious places on earth and billions of things exist that are smaller than pinheads and as large as blue whales. Every so often we get lucky and meet a new one."

I said, "Do you have that photo, the one you shot?"

Carroll nodded and went forward. I followed. He ducked into the wheelhouse, and there on the port bulkhead was a framed black-and-white picture, faded with age.

Staring at it, I said, "The one I saw was smaller but it looks like the same thing."

Carroll smiled. "Does it look like a clay model to you?"

"No."

"Guess where I shot that picture."

"Somewhere off here?"

The swordfisher nodded. "Two miles south, three miles west. Now let me show you a clipping from *The Professional Fisherman*, last month's edition."

SEA SOUND MYSTIFIES RESEARCH SCIENTISTS

A massive heartbeatlike thumping sound has been recorded by professional divers in waters off Dana Point, California, mystifying scientists from the Naval Undersea Research Institute. They admit, "We hear the signal, and we're staring at it and listening to it, trying to figure out what it is. We know it's alive . . ."

Carroll had a gleam in his eyes. "It's out there. *Out there!* So hang in, Danny. Someday we'll both be proved not to be liars."

The fish-nibbled body of Jack Stokes was recovered the next day: It had drifted north about ten miles. Preliminary tests on the blood found on the *Lotta Fun* indicated it did not belong to Jack Stokes. The *Times* reported that according to the medical examiner's office, it wasn't human blood.

Not human blood? Another mystery of the sea was added to the ageless list.

A day later, one so clear that the low mountains to the east could be seen, Buck and I went past the Dana Point jetties, outbound. In the *Spanker* locker was my dad's camcorder and my Vivitar 320Z, Power Zoom. Both had full loads of film. A rubber raft was also aboard for scale purposes.

We were outbound to drift-fish for sand bass and halibut, and to see what we could see.

Hating Hansen

*I*t happened fast to Bates, of Boone, North Carolina, a raw apprentice seaman aboard the American freighter SS *Mackinaw*. It happened like lightning or the shot of a gun. He plunged downward and was swallowed up by the cold sea in the far approaches to the English Channel.

The suck of the hull drew him cruelly along below the waterline, knifing him on barnacles—finally to release its hold, shunting him astern and to the surface of the white-water wake.

Bleeding from the scratches on his hands, right arm, and right side, he floated limply, with his head rolling loose around the collar of his life jacket. He was soon a mere chip in tumbling waves.

His eyes opened. He flailed out. His scream was tossed into the wind and roaring spindrift but he knew it was useless. The bobbing, twisting stern light of the *Mackinaw* was now but a dot on the black horizon, appearing and disappearing as the waves lifted and dropped the vanishing ship.

He laid his head back on the neck roll of the life

jacket and looked up at the sky that occasionally opened through low, scudding clouds, and prayed.

Was this the way he'd die, at the age of seventeen? Would it be two hours until he died of exposure? Maybe only one? Dawn was an hour away, he believed. Why, oh why, did he want to go to sea? Why, oh why, had he lied to the Coast Guard about his age, saying he was eighteen instead of seventeen?

Actually, he looked even older, bigger, than eighteen.

Then he remembered how it happened: Hansen, the pockmarked boatswain, chief of the deck gang, had stood by the starboard wing of the bridge, a small figure in foul-weather gear. For reasons unknown to Bates, Hansen had been his enemy since he boarded the *Mackinaw* eight months earlier. Tough, bantam rooster Olaf Hansen had picked on him daily, it seemed. Goaded him. Cursed him. Bates had asked older hands about the treatment and was told, "That's just his style. Let it roll off you, farm boy." Easy said.

"Bates, lash a sextant and chronometer in Number 1 boat," Hansen had yelled over the storm's howl. "Cap'n says we may have to abandon ship." He'd just come out of the wheelhouse. The *Mack* had had diesel trouble since midway across the Atlantic, shutting down twice. Without power, she could broach, turn over, in the huge waves.

The lifeboat had already been swung outboard, rigged in against the pudding boom, making it easier and quicker to launch.

Bates looked at it fearfully. The lifeboat was vibrating and dancing on each toiling roll of the ship.

It strained upward when a heavy swell washed the length of the *Mackinaw*.

"Better get someone to help me, Hansen," Bates shouted back. He'd need both hands to crawl out to the boat. He couldn't handle the wooden sextant and navigation-clock boxes at the same time.

Hansen stared from beneath the yellow sou'wester that crowned his head. His wet face gleamed; his pale blue eyes scoured Bates. "They're all busy," he shouted, waving toward the cluster of men on the foredeck. There were three big trailers lashed up there. Extra lines were being placed to keep them in position. Bates knew that Hansen was headed up there to supervise.

"I'll need help," Bates insisted.

The boatswain spat his disgust. "I'll help, dammit. Just get the sextant and the clock."

Bates could feel the dislike, even hatred, in Hansen's voice. It was naked this predawn; unreasoning, as it had always been. He'd been told by the older hands that this was Hansen's way of training his apprentice seamen. Bates had been on the 1600 to 2000 lookout watch when the storm roared in suddenly last night. Now he was on the morning 0400 to 0800.

Bates reached into the bridge locker and pulled out a length of line, then put the sextant and clock boxes under his arm. He lurched toward the ladder to the boat deck with Hansen close behind him. The boatswain followed and stood by the rear davit.

Bates waited until the *Mackinaw* righted itself, then he clambered out onto the lifeboat. He crouched down by the outer gunwale, looking cautiously at the frenzied water below. He glanced at Hansen and their eyes locked. He saw a half smile on the wizened face; he actually dreaded it. Hansen's eyes seemed to be saying, *How's this for training, you scared overgrown punk?*

Placing one end of the line under his knee, Bates quickly shoved the small wooden boxes that Hansen had passed him under a thwart and began to take turns around the seat, securing them beneath it. The wind tugged at his body, bulky in the life jacket, and he felt the lifeboat quivering.

He heard Hansen yell a warning and jacked his head around to look forward. A roller, spuming and thundering, piled toward the *Mackinaw*. His hands clutched the thwart.

The last he saw was Hansen's face, blue eyes staring. Then he felt his body arc into the air, and the space beneath him opened. It was that quick.

Then the water and the cruel barnacles; the rolling, buffeting waves; the cutting spray.

Floating, he again thought that no one should have to die this way. But for the Hansens of the world, no one would have to die this way. Die, hell! This was murder! His own deep hatred of Hansen boiled up in his mouth and he vomited. Maybe the hatred of Hansen could keep him alive.

The wind began to lower at first light and he floated wearily, his body chilling steadily. He made no effort to go anywhere. Why try? He'd just go to sleep and never wake up.

He wondered if the *Mackinaw* had stopped again and broached. Maybe they were all in the lifeboats. In a way that was comforting, because he liked most of the men on the *Mack*.

Before long he slipped off, submitting to weakness and a deep desire to sleep. Time passed, and he bobbed on the waves as the sunless gray light widened.

A sound awakened him, a *splat-splat-splat* like the blade of a prop on a ship riding high without cargo. He kicked his feet to bring his head higher and saw a black shape, downwind, with the familiar red running light; lights from portholes shone from beneath the bridge.

Frantically, he sought the button on the life jacket's small light. The white eye turned on. He remembered Hansen telling the apprentices how to do that and blow the overboard whistle. He yelled feebly, his breath coming in heaves as he tried to scull toward the shape. Soon a stream of light struck his face and stayed there, blinding him. He lay back in the long swell, exhausted.

Finally he felt strong hands pull him into a boat. Then blows were striking his face, slaps; but he felt no pain. His body was a rag doll and he felt it being lifted up. He passed out.

Some time later, he awakened with a form hovering over him. Something liquid burned down his throat and he coughed it up.

"You're a lucky boy," a voice said.

Bates made no effort to answer.

"What ship you off of?" the voice persisted.

"*Mackinaw*, American."

"You're aboard the *Dillery*. We're British. You can only thank God . . ."

Was this a dream? He slipped off into unconsciousness again and did not awaken for almost seven hours. Under several blankets, he was in crew's quarters. A pair of pants and a shirt were on the end of his bunk. He dressed and painfully made his way topside, where he asked the *Dillery's* chief mate, "Do you know what happened to the *Mackinaw*? Did she sink?"

"Rest easy, son. She's all right. Into Portsmouth several hours ago. We radioed her, told her we'd pick you up."

"Thank you," Bates murmured. "Where is this ship going?"

"Into Portsmouth, too."

Every muscle and joint ached, but he wanted to see the expression on Hansen's face when he re-boarded the *Mackinaw*. He wanted to hear what the rotten, murdering boatswain would say. He wanted to grind his fist into Hansen's pockmarked face.

The *Dillery* finally snugged alongside dock hours later, and Bates, refreshed from another long sleep, walked off her in a borrowed oversized wool sweater and a new pair of khaki pants.

Through the forest of cargo booms and kingposts, he could see the squatty gray-white stack of the *Mackinaw*. He made his way to the ship and slowly, almost mechanically, climbed the gangway, sweeping the deck for the sight of Hansen. Instead, he saw Second Mate McCall over by Number 4 hatch, where cargo was being lifted out of the hold.

He walked over to McCall, who extended his hand and said, "Thought we'd lost you . . ."

Bates nodded. "That's what I thought, too. Where's Hansen?" He was usually on deck when cargo was being worked.

McCall hesitated a moment, examining Bates's face. "He drowned. He dived after you and tried to rescue you."

"Are you kidding me?"

"I wish I was. Good man, Hansen."

Bates felt his knees buckling and sat down on a bitt.

The Butcher

*M*ichael Trinity was ten years old when his father, Malcolm, was murdered, in cold blood, in the home waters off Coolgardie, South Australia. His father was an abalone diver, wearing a home-sewn wet suit, rubber gloves, and homemade scuba gear. This was in 1949, in the early days of commercial abalone diving—before Australia developed a worldwide market for "abs"—and there was nothing to protect men like Malcolm from sharks.

All he had in his hands when the great white attacked was his abalone iron, used to pry the "black-lips" or "greenlips" from their rock homes on the grassy bottom. His burlap bag to haul them to the surface was attached to his waist; his scuba tank was harnessed over his back.

On the surface, Michael's tanned mother, Mary, was manning their work boat, the thirty-two-foot *Galah*, and standing by to pull up the abalone bag when his father signaled it was full. She loved her job, loved being out with her husband.

The great white struck without warning, as it did

most of the time. The two-inch, serrated triangular teeth, set in a mouth twenty-eight inches wide, cut Malcolm Trinity in two as if he'd been on a railroad track, as if a huge log saw had crossed his midriff.

Usually great whites do not eat their human victims, preferring sea lions, porpoises, dolphins, or big tuna. Having killed only for sport this time, the great white continued prowling his territory at the foot of Spencer Gulf, which lies between Wallaroo and the Eyre Peninsula.

The calm sea was like a sheet of gold that day, the weather mild. The first that Michael's mother knew something terrible had happened forty to fifty feet beneath the *Galah* was when she saw the large rusty stain of blood off the port side.

She frantically jerked the lifeline that he always rigged and attached to his waist when he dove. It was alongside the weighted line for the burlap bag. She began hauling on the lifeline. Just the feel of it, deadweight with no resistance, no responding jerks from her husband, caused her heart to slam.

Malcolm was still alive when she pulled him to the surface alongside the *Galah*, and she ripped off his scuba mask. He survived long enough to murmur, "Great white . . ." Then his chin sank down onto his breastbone. At the age of thirty-four, Michael's handsome, rugged, blond-haired father would never pry another ab, never draw another breath, never laugh heartily again.

At 105 pounds, Mary did not have the strength to haul him up and over the railing, but she tied him off under the armpits and, trailing blood, towed what was left of him into the harbor—refusing to look at the half corpse, wanting to remember him the way he was: a big, burly, yet gentle man, usually with a wide smile and a hug for almost everyone.

There, at the *Galah's* berth, fishermen and fellow ab divers took over the sad task of lifting the remains from the water. One walked Mary to the Trinity cottage, an arm tight around her shoulders.

Michael learned of his father's death when he came home from school, book sack over his shoulder. Three women were seated in the tidy front room and another was with his mother in the bedroom. The women all had somber faces and two were red eyed. They all looked at each other when he asked, "What's wrong?"

One finally said, "Something has happened to your dad, Michael."

He asked, "Where is Mum?" He thought the boat might have sunk.

The same woman replied, "In the bedroom."

Before he went in to Mary, he asked, "What happened?"

"She thinks a great white—"

An ab widow was more specific. "The Butcher did it, Michael, I'm certain."

He'd heard about the Butcher for years. He'd heard so much that he was even afraid of the name.

He knew the Butcher ruled the sea from the head of the Bight east to Wedge Island.

From the time that he was a small child he'd also known that his father, like many men of Coolgardie, had a dangerous job. He'd known that Malcolm risked his life every time he dived, but that his father would have no other life. He enjoyed bringing the abs up from the bottom. The money would never make them wealthy, but it was enough to feed and clothe them, make the monthly payments on the *Galah* and on their small house; enough for his father to have a pint of ale every night in his undershirt and suspenders.

Michael loved his father deeply. He went into the bedroom and sat down on the edge of the mattress. His mother and Michael put their arms around each other and wept for a long time. Wept until it hurt.

When he came out of that bedroom he vowed to someday murder the Butcher, as the Butcher had murdered his father.

Malcolm Trinity had left them his good name and his reputation as a brave and hardworking man. Aside from those priceless gifts, he left them very little. Michael's mother went to work as a waitress, and Michael did odd jobs around town and down in the harbor. They leased the *Galah* to a local ab diver who had lost his boat to an explosion and fire off Flinder's Island. The boat had burned down to the waterline. Just going to sea could be dangerous.

Over the next years, while he was growing up, there were times when Michael and his mother talked about moving to another city, going to Adelaide or Melbourne, but Coolgardie, where his father was born, held them. It was a close, friendly town, populated with their kind of simple people. And, of course, the spirit of Malcolm Trinity, if not the body, was out there in the chill water, night and day.

Over those years Michael did not forget his vow to kill the Butcher. During that time Michael tried to talk to every diver or fisherman who'd seen what they thought was the Butcher. The best estimate he had was a length of eighteen to twenty-one feet and a weight of up to three tons. Two fishermen had said they'd seen his dorsal fin, the curved part that is sometimes seen above the surface, estimating that it was almost four feet tall. The fin alone could cripple a diver.

He often walked along the edges of the lonely high sea cliffs west of Coolgardie, his father's binoculars in hand. He searched the swells, hoping to catch a glimpse of that huge dorsal fin, but he never did sight it.

Meanwhile, three more ab men had been lost and there was little doubt in town about their fates and the beast that had caused the tragedies. Frightened, several ab divers went to work on prawn boats fishing Spencer Gulf; several more moved up the coast to Woolengong and Taree to make their living. The Butcher ruled the depths.

Nightmares came now and then. They were horrible. Michael saw his father with nothing beneath his waist. He saw his father's face with terror on it. His screams awakened his mother. The dreams still occurred in his midteens.

Despite the dreams, the sea steadily drew Michael toward it, as it had drawn his father. He saved enough money to buy early Japanese scuba gear and dove along the reefs near Port Lincoln. From the moment he backed into the water and cleared the low surf, then rolled over to look down into the shallows for fish, the great white was on his mind.

His mother, who had not gone near the docks, much less a boat, since that noon of the Butcher, urged him to try tennis or track. "I bet you'd be a fine runner. There are so many wonderful things to do on land."

"I know that, Mum," he said, and added, for her sake, "I stay in shallow water."

She wasn't the kind of mother who harped on anything, but the look in her brown eyes when he went out the door with the mask, tank, wet suit, and spear was almost desperate.

Finally, when he was nineteen he called the University of Adelaide to talk to the professor who was supposed to be Australia's foremost expert on great whites. On the phone he told her he was from Coolgardie, the fishing village, and was interested in the great whites; that he was doing a school paper on them—a lie, of course. She agreed to talk to him, and he drove seven hours to Adelaide in his father's old British Ford pickup.

Dr. Alice Woolstenhume, a stocky lady in her midforties with close-cropped hair, was very friendly. "Now, what do you want to know?" she asked.

"Well, everything, Dr. Woolstenhume," he replied.

"People around here call me Dr. Alice."

"Everything, Dr. Alice."

She laughed. "Do you have ten years for this paper of yours?"

They talked for a long while. He learned from her that the great whites probably date back a hundred million years, to when most of Australia was still underwater, with maybe only the Macdonnell Ranges, in the middle of the country, sticking up. A type of great whites had hunted the marine megafauna of the primitive world. She said the great white might be the oldest true killer on earth.

He learned from the professor that the great whites have the finest hunting equipment in the sea world. Vibrations in the water up to six hundred feet away are sensed by nerve endings that spread through the massive body from nose to tail. The nerve ends signal the tiny brain, then the nostril system kicks in. The great white can sniff an ounce of blood in a million ounces of water.

They are born killers, Dr. Alice said, and the mother gives birth to as many as a hundred pups. "Most already have their teeth at birth and within an hour they are ready to defend themselves and hunt for food." Michael's mind pictured dozens of the sharklets going after helpless guppy-sized fish. Babies killing babies.

"They don't have air bladders and must move constantly or sink to the bottom and die. That's why they never sleep, though I think they doze at times."

He could picture the Butcher dozing in an underwater cave, his pectoral fins pumping slowly; after an hour's rest, emerging from the shadows for the almost endless patrol, nerve endings alert for movement ahead and on either side.

"They don't always attack, but when they do they first circle the victim at about ten feet, then turn, in a flash, and operate the massive jaws. As you likely know, the attacks are often in water no more than forty or fifty feet deep; in fact, usually less. Even waist-high water. I know of a case where a horse had been exercised in water ten or twelve inches deep; then the rider took him deeper, about four feet. Suddenly the horse was towed out to sea, minus the rider, and consumed. Imagine the terror of both the horse and the rider."

Just before he departed Dr. Alice's office, she said, "Why do I think you have something else on your mind?"

Why not tell her? Michael thought. She was so nice. He was ashamed he'd told her a lie. "I do," he admitted. "I plan to kill the Butcher. He murdered my father, an ab diver."

Though a frown flitted across her forehead, her voice remained unchanged. "I hope you've considered your plan carefully. It's a very dangerous undertaking.

"I have the name of your father in my file as a possible Butcher victim," she added.

Michael said, "I know it's dangerous."

"I spent several days on a chartered boat looking for him once. I was just as glad that I didn't find him," Dr. Alice said. "Frankly, I'm deathly afraid of him. You do have a plan?" She waited for him to give her an idea of what he had in mind.

Finally he said, "It's not quite formed." He had no plan, just the obsession.

She nodded. "When you're ready, please call me. Let's talk about it. I know he kills, but the Butcher is a magnificent great white specimen. I understand your feelings, still, I'd have very mixed feelings about someone ending his life. I'm a scientist, above all. . . ."

Several months passed, and one night Michael was half watching the telly when he looked over at Betty, their ancient canary. There she was, safe, in her cage. *That's it*, he thought. *A cage!* If he was in a steel cage, how could the Butcher get to him? And from the cage he'd find some way to kill him.

There was a trade and technical school run by the government in Port Lincoln, not far away. He called the next day and enrolled in a night welding class. In six weeks, he was a certified welder. It didn't take much brains or skill. He was not going to build an automobile, just cut and weld three-quarter-inch

steel re-bar, the round type used to reinforce con-
crete.

His mother was delighted that he had gone to
school to learn welding. He didn't tell her why.
They'd never talked about the possibility of him becoming an ab diver. Memory of the day his father
died was still much too painful for both of them.

He made a sketch of the cage he wanted to
build—six feet, six inches high, so he could stand
up; five feet square, so he could move around. The
diagonal steel bars would be no more than two feet
apart, so the Butcher could not get his mouth inside
the cage; the vertical steel bars would be no more
than twelve inches apart, for strength. The floor
would be steel re-bar every four inches; the roof
would be the same, except for a two-foot entryway.
A steel eye would be welded into the roof for the
steel cable from which the cage would dangle.

He made a copy of the sketch and sent it to Adelaide for Dr. Alice to check, asking if the three-
quarter re-bar would be strong enough to withstand
the great white's jaws. He wasn't sure she'd help
him, but she called back and said she thought the
welds, if done correctly, would hold. "But no one
has ever been able to figure just how much pressure
those jaws can exert or just what the tensile strength
is. I have an idea he can bite through a car roof like
it's tissue paper."

Then she had two questions: How did Michael
plan to kill the Butcher? And could she rig the cage
for automatic photographs?

As yet, he couldn't answer her first question. He
said OK to the second question.

"I still have very mixed feelings about what you
are trying to do. Truthfully, I'd like to take him

alive, put him in a huge tank, and study him. But I know that's impossible and I've already studied his brethren.

"I know he's a threat to any human and also an industry, yet I'm reluctant to help issue his death warrant."

Michael said, "I understand," but he didn't.

Word was out around Coolgardie about what Michael was trying to do, and the ab divers chipped in to help pay expenses. After figuring out how much re-bar he'd need, he hauled it home in the pickup, along with some rented welding equipment. At that point, with steel in the backyard, acetylene gas bottles, and a protective face helmet visible, he had to tell his mother.

"Please, Michael, please don't, please don't," she said. "That shark has caused enough hurt. I can't bear to lose you."

"I have to do it, Mum. Please understand."

"You don't *have* to do it at all. The attack wasn't personal. That shark just bit an ab diver. He didn't know it was your father. It could have happened to any diver that day."

Michael knew that. But the Butcher had robbed him of his father's life and that was very personal.

The subject came up several times over the next week, and neither of them budged as he completed the cage, bought the steel cable, and arranged to borrow the *Galah* from the diver who had leased it. She had a cargo boom and a small winch capable of handling the re-bar weight.

During this time Dr. Alice surprised him one evening. She called to say that a colleague of hers suggested placing an explosive charge into several

good-sized tuna. The Butcher might swallow them
and tear his guts out.

It seemed workable. Shooting him underwater
with a poison dart was sketchy. She said she'd have
the explosives and igniters put together at the university. Getting whole tuna in Adelaide was no problem. "And, Michael, I've thought about it a whole
lot. I'm going to be scared to death but I'd like to
go with you. I'll shoot the photographs myself."

"Thank you," he said, closing his eyes in grati-
tude. He was almost in tears. He wouldn't be facing
the Butcher alone.

The days passed rapidly. His next-to final chore
was to borrow two diving helmets and a compressor
from a Port Lincoln commercial outfit. He even
wound up with a volunteer professional, Jasper Perkins, to run the compressor and feed them the right
air/gas mixture.

Killing the Butcher had now almost become a
community project. Fishermen had been saving their
netted garbage catch, inedibles such as tommy
roughs and toadfish, to make fishgullion, a stinking,
slimy mess with sheep's blood added, to be dumped
into the current to flow back toward the cage—the
perfect enticer for a hungry great white. Ten five-
gallon red plastic buckets of fishgullion would go
into the pickup along with the cage.

On the afternoon before sailing on the shark hunt,
while he was grinding the fishgullion, his mother
surprised him. She said quietly, "I'm going with you
tomorrow. I'm taking the day off."

"Going with us? Mum, you sure about that?"

She nodded. "I think I can help you find him."

"You sure, Mum?"

She nodded again. He had no idea how she

thought she could help. But she did know the *Galah's* position when it all happened. She was a good sailor; a good helper; a courageous lady.

She was now forty years old, with premature gray hair and tired-lines in her face. He'd urged her to try and find another man. As a waitress, she served them six days a week, mostly predawn fishermen and ab divers. Her answer had been, "Who could possibly replace your father?"

Dr. Alice flew into Port Lincoln in early evening and they had dinner with Michael's mother: grilled whiting and new potatoes, fresh berries and ice cream. His mother talked about his father, at length, for the first time in years. Michael heard things, good things, that he had never known.

The harbor was quiet at gray dawn, except for a few work-boat engines and an idling sports-fisher diesel. The crayfish and prawn boats had left around 3:00 A.M. The air was chill, with a few patches of low-lying fog here and there over the water.

Michael took the *Galah* over to the fish dock, where his mother, Dr. Alice, and Jasper Perkins were waiting. The fish dock had a small electric crane and Michael used it to pluck the cage and the compressor from the pickup, placing them aboard in the long cockpit. Then they loaded the rest of the diving equipment, the ten five-gallon buckets of fishgullion, and the half dozen lethal tuna baits.

Dr. Alice's colleagues had gutted the blast-frozen tuna at the university, placed the charges inside, sewn them up, and rigged a pull string on each to start two-minute timers. The timers were taped to the charges—enough explosives to sever a wharf piling. Then they'd packed the tuna in a big cooler.

"What you really have are small depth charges, tiny replicas of the ones they use to destroy submarines. Just one should do the job, but you have five more if there's a malfunction."

"Suppose one blows up in the boat?" Jasper Perkins asked.

Dr. Alice smiled at him. "They'll be picking up fish scales and us for a quarter kilometer."

Michael steered between a reef that was an offshore home to great whites, and Hopkins Island, another haunt of theirs, and went out into open sea, leaving Spencer Gulf.

"Steer west," his mother said.

He turned the bow of the *Galah* to parallel the desolate, high brown shore cliffs, certain his mother was returning the boat to the area where his father had been killed. Fish, like many animals including humans, do have home territories, though they'll stray miles away on occasion.

As they motored west Michael kept checking the fish finder, getting readings of from forty to sixty feet; ab water on occasions when bottom rocks were plentiful. The inshore waters were comparatively shallow until the drop-off to the Great Australian Bight, where the depths plunged suddenly to six thousand feet or more.

In a light parka, Mary stood at the bow, looking now and then at the cliffs; getting a bearing, Michael knew. He watched her awhile, a tiny, silent figure; then he went forward. Before he could speak, she said, "He's up this way. I can feel his presence."

She'd never been a mystic, never believed in crystal balls; never been one of those women who close their eyes and go into trances to talk to spirits. "OK, Mum," he said, "just let us know when we can start dumping a bucket.'' The slime buckets were at the stern. He went back to the wheel.

About an hour and a half later, she suddenly turned and looked at him, eyes wide, face haunted, then pointed off the port bow. Dr. Alice frowned at him and he frowned back. They saw nothing. No huge dorsal fin slicing the water.

The morning sun was spanking off the blue-green sea. There was a slight chop. But the longer he looked, the more he felt a dread. False alarm? Mum's hopes?

She was still staring in the same direction and he said to both Dr. Alice and Jasper Perkins, ''Let's try here.''

Stopping the *Galah*, letting her drift, they got into the wet suits and he used the boom to lift the cage, with its tuna cargo, and dangle it over the stern. He tied it off temporarily.

Michael walked forward again, to stand beside his mother. ''You still feel him?''

Face ghostly white, she murmured, ''Yes.''

He geared the motor in again and turned due south, with just a few revs for steerage. He pried the lid off the first fishgullion bucket and dumped it over the side, then went into reverse. The current was setting toward shore. He dropped the anchor.

He asked Jasper to dump a bucket every half hour, a little at a time.

''Ready to go?'' he asked Dr. Alice.

She nodded and they put on the helmets, the air/gas flowing into the hoses. They climbed into the cage, close quarters, and Jasper worked the winch to lower them to about thirty feet, halfway to the bottom. They'd tied six-ounce weights to the tuna so they wouldn't skid away or float up.

Back-to-back in the cold blue-greenness, descending slowly, all they could see were schools of pipefish and cowfish, and some tommy roughs, attracted by the slime. Vision laterally was about forty feet, light from the strong sun reaching down that far. After that, in each direction, murk began to set in. Dr. Alice adjusted her underwater Nikon.

His heart pounding, mouth dry, as they slowly swung back and forth in the cage he'd welded, Michael suddenly felt very vulnerable. He fought off seasickness. They had invaded the Butcher's property and he did not know if his welds would hold under all-out attack. The jaws of a six-thousand-pound creature had that unknown strength Dr. Alice had talked about. And even if the welds held, by accident or on purpose the Butcher could easily snap the air hoses to both helmets. They could hold their breath for about eighty seconds, then they'd have to dump the helmets and swim up, exposed to a raging white until they clambered into the boat. He had visions of him following them up, jaws closing as they had on his father.

Time seemed endless; there was nothing to do but wait. Jasper dumped a second bucket, dribbling it out; then a third. After an hour and a half of standing and waiting, they were both chilled and stiff. Michael pulled on the signal line, which rang a small bell, and Jasper heaved them up with the winch.

As soon as the helmets came off, Jasper said, "You see any sharks?"

Dr. Alice answered, "A few little bullheads. They make meals for the whites."

Though the sun was warm, they shivered pulling off the wet suits, and Michael asked his mother, "You still think he's around here?"

"I do," she said confidently.

Michael was beginning to think it was a fool's trip, a waste of time. But he suspected that feeling was caused by fear.

Sitting in the sun, cold and wet, Michael and Dr. Alice drank several cups of hot coffee and ate sandwiches, not talking much.

Jasper fed another bucket of the oily fish waste into the water.

They'd been up on deck for about forty-five minutes when Mary said tightly, "There . . ."

She was pointing almost dead ahead. A dorsal fin the size of a house door was crossing the *Galah's* bow, creating a V-wave. Then it submerged like a submarine's conning tower.

"My god," Dr. Alice said, and Michael joined her remark silently, grabbing for a new wet suit. Dropping half her sandwich into the sea, Dr. Alice did the same.

To keep the shark interested and close by, Jasper tilted two more buckets while they helmeted up and got into the cage again at surface level. If Michael's heart had pounded before, if fear had almost made him puke, his heart was now beating inside his ears like a kettledrum. Inside the helmet he was almost panting with fright. He had no reason to believe that the professor wasn't doing the same. Her camera was ready.

As they again swung at thirty feet below, he reached down to cut the fish line holding the lead weights and lifted one tuna, holding it between his knees; he did the same to another but held it in his hands.

It seemed forever and forever before the Butcher emerged out of the murk and came toward them like a gray torpedo, aiming his giant head and totally black eyes, large as teacups, at the cage. There were rage wrinkles extending above his open mouth, and his saw-blade teeth were in attack mode.

He hit the cage like a locomotive and knocked it on its side, so that Michael was lying on top Dr. Alice for a few seconds. Then the cage swung back violently, several of the tuna sliding outside it. They seemed to be enclosed in bubbles and turbulence.

Later he wouldn't remember doing it, but he jerked the strings on two more of the fish and shot them out of the cage, between the bars, hoping their timers started.

The Butcher attacked again, his huge teeth actually grabbing the steel bars, his angry head within inches of them, twisting as if to tear them apart. Michael knew Dr. Alice was clicking away with the Nikon, steadying herself with an elbow against his shoulder.

He managed to jerk the timer string on another tuna, sending it out of the cage, pulling on the signal line to Jasper at the same time, yelling into the helmet phone, "Get us out of here, Jasper, for God's sake get us out of here . . ."

Then they began to move upward, all too slowly, and the great white took one last whack at them, as enraged as he was on the first locomotive strike. Michael had never seen such an angry, frustrated face. The cage went on its side one last time, smashing them against the bars.

As they emerged into the glorious sunlight, they heard a dull thud from below, and by the time they crawled out of the cage, so weak they couldn't talk, rusty stains of blood were coming up around the *Galah*, followed by bits of the Butcher.

The Schoolie

*S*tanding on the starboard bridge wing of the SS *Morning Light*, which he'd boarded three hours previously, Jack Mako took a long look over the gasoline tanker's well deck, with its maze of piping, toward her blocky afterhouse and high old-fashioned stack. He immediately thought she was no ship to labor through a hurricane, and in the soft illumination of the dock lights his young face showed concern.

Under straw-colored hair, it was a clean, cultured face, with a solid chin—in contrast to the *Morning Light*, in which nothing seemed solid. He'd just graduated from the U.S. Merchant Marine Academy. He had his third mate's license from the Coast Guard and this would be his maiden voyage as an officer. He'd passed his twenty-second birthday two months ago.

Before climbing to the bridge he'd made a guess that the *Morning Light* had had at least thirty years of plying the oil runs to Texas and Venezuela and the West Indies petroleum ports. The catwalk had a buckle in it. A bulky 490 feet long, 6,800 tons, she still had gun tubs, empty now, from fighting the Nazis in World War II.

Old as she was, she might well crack her plates in the gray-green seas of Hurricane Babs, which was flattening Barbados, Grenada, and Carricou this very moment, after coming up out of the South Atlantic. It didn't take an old salt to know that.

The Miami Hurricane Center was predicting that Babs would travel slowly due west, then swing north, strengthening into a hundred-mph storm within forty-eight hours. Babs was described as "extremely dangerous." All shipping in the Caribbean was being warned. Just his luck to sail when the vicious lady called Babs was roaring around.

Despite the weather, the *Morning Light* was still loading auto gas into her twelve cavernous tanks, topping off. The cargo had been coming aboard fore and aft for the last twelve hours.

Mako glanced at Captain Einer Sarninen, who had his elbows on the bridge wing railing, occasionally looking toward the bow, anxious to get under way from the Dutch West Indies port of Curaçao. Wisps of thick, unruly silver-streaked black hair curled from beneath his scrambled-egg hat, which was soiled and battered. He had a blocky face capped by bushy salt-and-pepper eyebrows. His eyes seemed to rest, in their depths, on blue glacial plateaus. Mako reckoned him to be physically powerful.

Mako hadn't met too many ships' masters. He'd been a summer deck cadet on two freighters, but this would be only his third voyage.

Sarninen's attention was suddenly drawn to the gangway, which connected the *Morning Light* to land. "Look at that spectacle," he muttered, his slight Finnish accent turning his *ts* to *ds*.

Mako was already looking. A man was down on his hands and knees midway up the slotted gangway, laid out a few paces behind the bridgehouse. Obviously drunk, the runty man in a rumpled, sweaty khaki shirt and stained pants was quite helpless. Yet, at the head of the gangway, McKelvy, the boatswain, stripped to the waist, was making no effort to help him up. He yelled at the groveling form, "Thought you wasn't goin' to make it, Cajun. But this is home, ain't it?" Then he hooted foul, disparaging laughter.

Sarninen yelled at the gangway, "Ca-j-u-n-n-n." It came out with a roll, like a dog call, the last syllable lingering in the thick, acrid air that hung over the Curacaosche Petroleum Maatschappij refinery area. Sarninen observed the scene for a moment longer, then growled down to the husky seaman: "Help him, bo'sun, so we can get under way."

The boatswain glanced at Sarninen with disappointment. He wanted more fun. But he moved, with a careless shrug, down the gang and practically yanked the man known as Cajun aboard. He stood him up erect and laughingly pointed him aft. That done, the bo'sun—whom Mako disliked already— yelled for help dragging the gangway in. Cajun weaved back through snaking pipelines to the crew's quarters.

Sarninen watched him go, then said to Mako, "That, Mr. Mako, is my messboy. Your messboy, too. He's really a remarkable animal. He's from New Orleans and can hold almost as much liquor as these tanks. Used to be a waiter on Mississippi cruise boats. Gets drunk in every port, and I sometimes hope he'll miss the ship. But he never does. He's my pet albatross."

Being addressed as "Mr." bothered Mako, but he knew it was sea etiquette. "Why do you keep him on, Cap'n?"

Sarninen's eyes lit up and he laughed gutturally. "When I was a boy in Helsinki, I read much about kings and courts. A jester is needed here more than in a palace." Then he laughed so hard that tears came into his eyes.

Mako felt his stomach flop; the laugh had a disturbing quality about it, a *whah-whah-whah* sound, an almost animal sound. Then he looked aft again as Cajun rotated foggily before the tank hatch on the far starboard side of the well deck.

Sarninen moved away from the railing, suddenly becoming authoritative. "All right, Mr. Mako, tell the second mate to single up all lines aft; tell the chief to hold the bow spring line." Then he stood back to observe his new third mate, looking from his new hat down to his shining shoe tips. "If everyone agrees, I'd soon like to get out of here, and on the road to Philadelphia."

That's more like it, Mako thought. Perhaps the *Morning Light* was only a sick ship in port. Using the loud hailer, he issued the orders.

Then Sarninen chuckled again in retrospect. "Cajun'll sober up in the morning," he said. "I had the chief mate lock Cajun's cabin when he left the ship. He always hides a jug in there." "Jug" was pronounced "yoog."

While they were waiting for the big loading hoses to be disconnected, Sarninen surveyed the dark, starry skies. "Did you check the weather?"

"Yes, sir. If we go on the course you laid out,

Cap'n, we'll cross the hurricane—if it keeps on westing.''

Sarninen again held the young third in a probing gaze for at least ten seconds. "Mr. Mako, I don't change course unless I'm going to hit another ship or run aground. I don't change course for weather unless I know it will break me up. 'Know' is the word I said. Positive knowledge, Mr. Mako. We'll go north through Windward Passage."

Mako frowned, then nodded.

"Were you taught at King's Point that to alter course can cost you several days' sailing time and thousands of dollars?" Sarninen asked.

"Yes, sir, I was," Mako said. He'd also been taught that altering course might save your ship.

A moment later the bridge telephone rang and Mako answered, then relayed the message to Sarninen. "Cajun's causing trouble in the crew's mess."

Sarninen grinned inexplicably and seemed pleased. "You might as well learn something about your new shipmates. Go back there and make peace, Mr. Mako."

Mako hurried down the ladder to the catwalk, his feet chopping at the steel rungs, wondering if this were normal procedure. He ran aft in long strides, quickly descending another ladder to the well deck, entering the lower starboard passageway of the afterhouse. He made a guess as to the location of the crew's mess.

Mako soon found himself in the doorway and looked inside. It was a room about fifty feet square with a half dozen wooden tables, a large pantry, and a half-gate serving area. Cajun was standing in the forward section, a fire ax in his hands. His pudgy, pasty potato face was vacant rather than threatening, and his eyes were glazed.

Cox, the seaman Mako had met when he first came aboard, sat unconcernedly at a table across the room, one big hand around a coffee mug. Another sailor was sitting beside Cox.

They glanced over at Mako, surprised.

Cajun said, "Who lock mah door?"

Cox grinned. "Beats me, Cajun."

"Somebody lock it."

"Maybe you did," suggested Cox.

Cajun shook his gray-stubbled head. "Naw, naw . . ."

"Put the ax down before you cut yourself," Cox advised lightly.

"I'm gonna chop it down," Cajun suddenly decided.

Cox grinned again. "But if you break it down, Cajun, then somebody could steal everything you've got."

"Thass right," Cajun muttered, "but nobody's gonna lock mah door. Nobody."

Mako was startled by the swift movement of the ax. It crashed into the tabletop nearest Cajun, and splinters flew. Cox leaped to his feet, the smile vanishing. The other sailor retreated into the pantry.

"Cut it out, Cajun," Cox yelled.

Mako moved quickly. He stepped into the room. "Put it down, Cajun," he ordered quietly.

Cajun glanced up. "Who you?"

"You've had your fun, Cajun. Give me the ax," Mako said, holding out his right hand and advancing a step.

Cajun cocked his head to one side, attempting to focus on the new third mate. "You lock mah door?"

"No, Cajun," Mako said warmly. "I flew in from New York tonight. My name is Jack Mako. I'm replacing Mr. Suarez."

Cajun's eyes focused. His small mouth became purposeful as Mako inched forward. "You know," Mako said soothingly, "Mr. Suarez took a shore job."

Then the expression on Cajun's face changed and Mako saw the ax blade coming at him in a murderous arc. He dodged back and edged into the doorway.

Mako glanced over his shoulder and saw that the bo'sun had unrigged a passageway fire hose.

Cox spotted the bo'sun and yelled, "Don't come in, McKelvy. Cajun's gone crazy."

McKelvy nodded and looked at Mako. "We'll hit him with this. I had the engine room build up sixty pounds on the line."

"Not yet," Mako said, watching the messboy.

Inside, they could hear the ax crunch into another tabletop.

"Mate, you gonna let him chop the room up?" McKelvy asked coldly.

The bo'sun had pulled a dirty undershirt over his wide shoulders. Mako judged him to be in his late twenties. He had small eyes set under heavy brows, high cheekbones, and a big nose.

Mako pondered. It wasn't very likely they could take Cajun any other way.

"Okay, Boats, let's hit him." Then he grabbed the hose just below the nozzle and pointed it at Cajun. McKelvy jerked down on the valve handle. The solid stream of water slammed the messboy in his chest, driving him back over a splintered tabletop. Cajun, wheeling in a tumble of arms and legs, struck his head on another table and sagged unconscious to the deck.

Mako grimaced, but McKelvy grinned triumphantly. "Simple, huh?"

"Yeah, Boats," Mako grunted.

Then he knelt over Cajun. The messboy was out cold, a red welt growing on his forehead. "All right, McKelvy, take him to his bunk. I think the chief mate's got the key to his room."

Mako looked around. Three tables were destroyed. Out of the corner of his eye, he saw McKelvy pull Cajun up by his collar. "Not so rough!" he shouted angrily.

McKelvy grinned again. "He can't feel a solitary thing, Mate." Then he swung the sodden mass up over his shoulders and started out.

The phone rang. "Cap'n says he wants Cajun up on the bridge," Cox reported.

Cox ran a hand over a splintered tabletop. "This'll cost him," he said.

Mako sighed. "A lot of people around here seem to get pleasure out of kicking this guy."

Cox walked back to his coffee mug and picked it up. "He's almost a halfwit, Mate. Drinks too much, but he's harmless."

Remembering the keening of the ax blade, Mako said, "I'm not sure he's harmless."

"I feel sorry for him."

"So do I," Mako replied, and then hurried along the passageway and across the catwalk. On the upper bridge level, to the rear of the wheelhouse, he could see the wavering beam of a flashlight and several figures knotted in a shadowy bunch.

As he neared them, he could make out the captain and McKelvy, along with the lifeless body of Cajun,

hunched down by the after bridge pipe railing. It was
a strange place for a reprimand, Mako thought. He
hurried up the two levels, meeting the helmsman on
the ladder to the bridge wing. He was carrying a
bucket of water.

"What's that for?" Mako asked.

"For Cajun. Ice water."

"You mean he's going to douse him?"

The helmsman nodded. Mako stuck a hand in the
pail. The water stung. This was 1956, not 1856.
"Throw that water over the side and draw some regular tap water."

The helmsman stared anxiously at the taut face of
the new third officer, and then obediently stepped
forward of the lifeboat davit and emptied the bucket.
Then he ducked back inside the passageway to refill
it.

Mako continued up the ladder, turned the corner,
and saw Cajun. The messboy was sitting on the
deck, half conscious. The welt on his forehead had
turned blue. His wrists were manacled to the pipe
rail.

Sarninen glanced up. "This is my sobering chamber, Mr. Mako. Fresh air and cold water."

"It will probably work," Mako said quietly.

"It always works," Sarninen corrected.

The helmsman joined them with the bucket of water.

"Douse him," Sarninen ordered, and the water
sloshed down Cajun's rolling head and down across
his shoulders and back. Cajun groaned and tried to
come to his hands and knees but the manacles re-
strained him. Sarninen, with the butt of his hand,
raised Cajun's head and then looked at the helms-

man. "This water's warm!" he roared. "I told you to use ice water."

Mako broke in quietly, his heart pounding. "I told him not to."

Captain Sarninen rose slowly and turned to Mako. He was incredulous. He shook his head, unable to believe what he'd just heard, and Mako stiffened for attack. "You . . . told . . . him . . . not . . . to."

Mako said evenly, "That's right, Cap'n."

The sun-mottled skin over Sarninen's forehead tightened perceptibly, and his lips peeled back as he sought words. "Mister, never countermand an order of mine. Never!" he finally bellowed.

"But, Cap'n, this man could get pneumonia out here."

Sarninen struggled to control himself. He stepped toward Mako. "Then it will be my concern," he said, his tone deadly. "But understand something and understand it before we leave the dock. Never countermand an order of mine. Understand that."

Then he turned to McKelvy. "Have someone throw ice water on him, every hour until dawn."

McKelvy nodded.

Sarninen swung back toward the new third mate. "Now, Mr. Mako, would it be possible to get this ship under way—if we can all agree?"

Mako replied, "Yes, Cap'n," and moved toward the ladder to the bridge deck, aware that the chunky Finn was following close behind.

"Give me slow astern when we're cast off," he heard Sarninen say.

Mako picked up the loud hailer and directed it aft. "Take in the stern spring line . . ."

A moment later, the bridge phone rang. "All clear aft."

Then the third ordered the forward spring lines to be taken in.

Sarninen muttered, "Let's go," and Mako stepped inside the wheelhouse and rotated the engine room telegraph back and forth, settling it to SLOW ASTERN. Then he felt the deck quiver as the *Morning Light's* propeller chewed into the Schottegat, the inner harbor. He reached up and heaved down on the whistle handle.

A long blast shattered the midnight quiet over the island of Curaçao.

The captain, Mako soon saw, was an expert seaman. He watched as the bow spring flipped off the dock and splashed with a white eruption before fishtailing into the ship. The *Morning Light* pulled away. The Dutch harbor pilot was aboard, to fulfill a legal formality; but it was Sarninen who handled her like a plaything. She backed out in an easy curve, and then Sarninen ordered Mako to put her on half speed for the run down Saint Anna Channel.

Soon the *Morning Light*, its afterhouse homey and warm with the glow of the porthole lights, slid past the famous pontoon bridge of the oil complex; and after dropping the harbor pilot, in a few minutes she was lifting gently to the first sea swells of the Caribbean, a rope of sooty smoke trailing from that grotesque stack, marring the moonlight.

Shortly after twelve-thirty, Mr. Fusari, the second mate, his chores done on the fantail, arrived on the bridge to take over the 12-to-4 watch, and Sarninen departed for his cabin a deck below.

"That's a pretty lousy thing, isn't it?" Mako said to Fusari. "The guy back there until dawn."

Fusari answered without sympathy. "There's a Cajun on every ship. He's durable."

Mako frowned at the second's callousness and left the bridge wing to go to bed, pausing to look at Cajun before descending the ladder.

Cajun didn't look durable. He was soaked and shivering in the trade wind that hummed across the deck. His chin was nestled on one shoulder. His eyes were closed, but his lips seemed to move. The wind that bore across the deck took his words, whatever they were, with it.

The shipping representative in New York hadn't revealed too much about the *Morning Light*. She was old and slow, he'd said. A torpedo had broken her back in World War II and she'd been welded back together. She was owned by a Greek company. When Mako had asked about her captain, the rep had said, "Sarninen's a master mariner but he's also a handful." Mako now knew that Einer Sarninen was more than a "handful."

Able-bodied seaman Cox had been at the gangway head and was visibly startled when Mako had walked up, introducing himself as the new third mate. Mako had been clad in Ivy Leagues, and his expensive leather bags displayed good taste. It was evident that the shipping rep had not forewarned those aboard the *Morning Light* to expect a collegiate. Cox had been pleasant, though, and had led him to the captain's in-port cabin. Mako had sat tensely before the raking eyes of Captain Sarninen, who had alternated examination of the license and certificates with personal examination of Jack Mako himself.

"First time on a tanker, huh?" Sarninen queried softly.

"Yes, sir."

"And a schoolie? You don't look over twenty," Sarninen had muttered. Mates who came up through the ranks always commanded more respect than maritime-school graduates.

Mako again said, "Yes, sir," trying to judge the captain's true attitude.

Sarninen had then dismissed him. "You can meet the other people later. But now go on up and check my courses to Philly." As Mako had departed the sparsely but meticulously furnished cabin, he'd carried Sarninen's eyes inserted into his back. And on the bridge, scanning the course that might steam them into the eye of Babs, Mako had realized that the captain was also trying to test him.

At 7:00 A.M., Chief Mate Elder Carson, a huge, balding man with a brimming belly and forearms the size of oak tap roots, was stepping off the course with dividers. Carson looked to be in his midforties or early fifties. They had not met the night before.

"Welcome aboard," Carson said. Then he gazed at Mako for a moment before saying, "I heard about you and Cajun."

"I made a mistake," Mako said.

"I think you did. You know what a sea lawyer is?"

"I've heard the term."

"A sea lawyer is a mate, engineer, or crew member who meddles in the ship's business, the captain's business, the company's business. They usually end up in trouble. Some end up overboard. On this ship, being a sea lawyer isn't very healthy."

Mako nodded. "I understand." Carson's very manner indicated he'd be a friend on this voyage.

Captain Sarninen yawned his way out of his sea cabin, which was on the bridge level, and came into the chart room.

"Morning, sir," Mako said.

Sarninen grunted sourly at the spick-and-span third. Mako knew he was still in trouble. What's more, he'd never get out of trouble on this ship.

"Mornin', Cap'n," Carson murmured.

"Mornin', Mate, you get a position?"

The beefy chief mate nodded. "A coupla stars at daybreak. We've been averagin' eight knots."

Less than a hundred miles since leaving Curaçao, Mako thought. *She* was *slow. Ancient turbines*.

Sarninen checked the predicted 8:00 A.M. position with a stubby index finger.

Carson continued, "These old engines are going to fly right out of this hull someday, you know . . ."

Sarninen interrupted rudely. "What's the latest on that hurricane, Mr. Carson?" Mako sensed there was little affection between them.

Carson shoved a piece of yellow paper from the radio shack toward the captain. "She's slowed down but we'll get a taste of it before we get to Windward Passage, I'd say."

Sarninen glanced at his first mate with disdain. "That's what you'd say, huh? I'd say by the time we get there, we'll only get a little rough sea."

Sarninen moved toward the door to the wheelhouse, then paused. "What time did you let Cajun off the bridge?"

"At dawn, as you ordered," Carson answered coldly.

Sarninen smiled. "Sober, I expect. Very sober and

very remorseful.'' He nodded to himself in satisfaction and went below to his in-port cabin.

Carson spoke into the emptiness of the doorway. ''I never disobey orders, Mr. Mako, but I did put a blanket on Cajun's shoulders when I went on watch.''

Mako looked at the big mate and smiled. Yes, he appeared to be a good man. He relieved Carson a few minutes before eight, ready to stand watch until noon.

The officer's mess of the *Morning Light* ran starboard to port on the upper deck, near the stern. On the forward bulkhead was a built-in mahogany sideboard, and the mess table itself was almost as long as the room. Captain Sarninen always sat at the starboard head of the table, and the foot was reserved for Joe Stern, the chief engineer, a white-haired, crook-backed, scrawny New Englander in his late sixties who usually met life, and Einer Sarninen, with a thoughtful chuckle.

Mako uneasily seated himself for the noon meal opposite Rodney, the third engineer, a sharp-visaged man of about thirty who wore his coveralls like a scarecrow. Fusari, fat and chin dimpled, had also come in for lunch, as well as Grosset, the brooding, silent second engineer.

''Welcome aboard, Mako,'' Rodney said. ''You're in for an interesting ride on this old scow. It should have been in the scrap yard ten years ago. Babs may twist us in half.''

Joe Stern had heard this kind of talk many times. ''It still floats, still runs.''

Mako noticed Cajun approaching the table with his soup. ''Remember me?'' he asked pleasantly.

The messboy frowned. He had on a waiter's white jacket that was wrinkled and frayed. He wore tennis shoes. Cajun shook his head. "Nah, sir."

"How do you feel?"

Cajun smiled back self-consciously. "Like I was drunk last night." The man from New Orleans was little more than five feet tall. His eyes were watery, set into unhealthy saffron skin that was bunched into a knobby nose, puffed cheeks, and receding chin. It was a troubled, harassed, bruised face. He was soft and his hands were pinkish, probably from food handling. The ravages of alcohol, and of the impalings he suffered from Sarninen and McKelvy, showed plainly in both his face and body. Mako guessed him to be about fifty, older than he'd appeared the previous night.

"You certainly were drunk," Mako said.

Joe Stern chuckled and chimed in from the end of the table. "I hear you took a bath last night."

Mako looked at Stern. The thin, hazy sun coming through the after bulkhead ports was spraying his white hair. Had Stern donned a black robe, he could have posed with the Supreme Court bench.

"He was *given* a bath last night, Chief," Mako said evenly. Since he'd already tangled with Sarninen on this, there was no need to hide his feelings.

Stern raised his eyebrows at Mako's obvious criticism. "Nobody fools with this skipper," he warned. "But nobody, boy."

Rodney looked up defiantly from his plate. "Somebody should." Then he said to Cajun, "First thing you do when we get back to Philadelphia is go to your union."

Pointing with his pipe, Stern interrupted. "Not so

fast. Do you want the old man to turn him in for habitual drunkenness?''

Cajun looked baffled by the debate and stood silently.

Mako wished he hadn't commented—another mistake.

"Nope, Cajun," Stern continued, "stay away from your union if you want to keep sailing. You deserved what you got last night. Take my advice and stay away from your union. You've been kicked off half the ships on the Atlantic seaboard. And remember, the skipper's been pretty good to you. You have a job."

Mako almost choked.

The little man in the frayed jacket looked at Rodney, then at Stern, and quickly retreated into the galley.

Silence settled over the mess until Rodney broke it. "The captain wants a helpless target, and Cajun fits it. Halfwitted, broke, drunk. The old man couldn't find a better piece of whipping human."

Mako wondered what he'd gotten into.

Sarninen stepped through the door, and Mako watched as he paused a moment to survey Rodney. He'd heard it all. Then the captain hung his hat on a rack by the sideboard, smoothed his granite-streaked hair, and took his seat.

"It's not so much what you said when I came in as what you said before I came in, Mr. Rodney."

Mako glanced at Rodney. He seemed unafraid. Before answering, Rodney ripped off a piece of bread and began chewing it casually. "I told Cajun he ought to report you to his union. And I might add, if it was me, to the Coast Guard as well."

Sarninen laughed and looked from the face of one officer to another.

Rodney added, "If you haven't already guessed, this is my first and last trip on this tub."

"My," the captain crooned, "things are getting out of hand. Last night it was my new third officer, a schoolie, who was interfering with my command . . ."

Mako met Sarninen's look head-on.

"This morning it's my third engineer. A man in your department, Joe," he added for Stern's benefit.

Joe Stern sucked noisily on his pipe but wanted no quarrel.

Captain Sarninen arranged his napkin on his lap formally and continued, enveloping them all in sarcasm: "I guess there just aren't enough duties to keep your minds occupied. The unions have fattened your paychecks, made your lives easier at sea, forced the company to fancy up this ship for your comfort." His tone turned icy. "But the matter of discipline, Mr. Rodney and Mr. Mako, they leave entirely to me."

Cajun emerged from the galley door, carrying the captain's salad.

"Captain, unfortunately you are right—but someday they'll catch up to you," Rodney said.

Sarninen waited until Cajun placed the salad in front of him. As soon as the plate settled, Sarninen, with a deliberate thumb, flipped it off the table, and it landed at Cajun's feet. The messboy stood dumbly, staring at the splattered greens. Mako watched his expression change from shock to bewilderment.

Sarninen said crisply, but with evident pleasure,

"You stuck your finger in my plate when you put it down."

Cajun mumbled, "Sorry, Cap'n," and bent over to begin scraping the contents back onto the plate.

Rodney scissored through the tense air. "Tell me, Captain, did you do that for my benefit?"

Grosset sighed and excused himself.

Sarninen glanced at Rodney briefly. "Yes, yours and that of anyone else in this room who does not understand that there can't be seven masters on a ship. There is one master and six officers."

The muscles in Rodney's thin jaw twitched, and a thin line of white rode his cheekbones. He rose, threw his napkin to the table angrily, and left.

Mako knew that it was now his turn. He could feel it coming.

"Mr. Mako, we should all start this voyage in agreement, shouldn't we?"

There was that word again. "Agree" to baiting and brutality?

Mako nodded and murmured, "Excuse me, sir," but Sarninen waved him back to his seat.

Fusari decided to depart.

Mako clamped his jaws and concentrated on his coffee. He was being humiliated and knew it.

Sarninen said to Stern, "This is a nice lad, Joe. I know one when I see one. First time I've ever had a schoolie on my vessel. He's a gentleman, not like your Rodney. I think he'll make a good officer."

Mako tried to shut his ears.

Sarninen grew pensive. "Joe, these young men don't think the way you and I do. Physically, they're equipped for sea. Mentally, no. Mr. Mako here, for instance, stepped out of bounds last night. And he, above all, being a schoolie, knows what imposed bounds are.''

''Times have changed,'' Stern observed.

Sarninen sighed. ''Yes,'' he agreed as Cajun brought a new salad in.

Stern got up, grumbling about old age. He tamped out his pipe. ''Ah, my rheumatism again.'' He massaged his bony shoulders. ''Hear we're going into a spot of weather.''

Sarninen passed it off lightly. ''We got a small duster working, Joe. Not much of anything to worry about. I think it will pass east of us.''

Cajun was hanging on every word, Mako saw. Babs had been discussed at breakfast.

''She can't take much weather anymore, Cap'n, and I'm too old to swim. She ain't the ship she was ten years ago when you came aboard. She's worn.''

''Still sound,'' Sarninen insisted.

''We both know the hull is weak around Number 5 tank, where she was torpedoed,'' Stern continued, stuffing his pipe into his jacket pocket. ''You love her, but don't expect too much from her.''

''I do love her. I also know her. I'm not going to put her in jeopardy. Nor am I going to dodge around some bad weather and cost the company two days' sailing time.''

There was a beat of silence. When Stern spoke again he didn't pursue the subject. ''See you later. I've got a pesky pump to tear down.''

After the chief engineer left, Mako asked, ''May I go now, Cap'n?''

Sarninen smiled. ''A few minutes more.''

Mako felt a throbbing in his temples. ''Cap'n, I apologize for last night.''

Sarninen nodded. ''You should. I know you are

not like the other scum on this ship. You're educated. You probably come from a good family.''

''I think so.''

''Your father does what?''

''Medical doctor, a cardiologist.''

''Your mother?''

''University professor, contemporary literature.''

''I read the classics . . .''

Mako rose. ''Cap'n, I have some chores . . .''

''What's keeping you?''

Mako managed to avoid the captain the rest of the afternoon, and ate early to avoid him at dinner. But on the evening 8-to-12 watch, his own watch, the captain stayed on the bridge for more than two hours without speaking. He sat in his high chair on the starboard wing and stared out into the night.

In the morning, when Mako crossed the catwalk to go to breakfast, he saw that the seas were becoming oily and there was a yellow tinge to the sky. This was, he remembered from meteorological classes, evidence of an approaching tropical disturbance. *Sarninen's terribly foolhardy*, he thought.

In the chart room, Chief Mate Carson was bent over the large hydrographic area map. ''I think we're going to be right in the eye of it if we keep this heading.''

''What was in the latest advisory?'' Mako asked.

''Nothing good. A navy hurricane hunter flew into it at dawn. Winds up to a hundred-ten miles an hour.''

''Maybe the old man will change his mind and run from it?''

''Not a chance. The Greeks give him a bonus if he keeps on schedule.''

Mako glanced at the chart. Carson was right. Another twenty-four hours and they'd be in the path of Babs. "But surely, losing a couple days . . ."

"Every day at sea means another day you can't get a new cargo aboard. You should have learned that at King's Point," Carson said.

"I did."

Captain Sarninen entered suddenly.

Carson glanced up. "This latest advisory, based on the 6:00 A.M. position, doesn't look good."

Sarninen eyed the chart. "No hurricane warning looks good."

"Do you want to check it?" Carson asked.

Sarninen frowned. "The storm is going to move more to the east," he said in a threatening voice. "Out of our path."

Mako listened, wise enough not to say anything.

"Not according to Miami," Carson said.

"Miami!" Sarninen snorted. "How many people in that glorified weather bureau have ever sailed this sea? I know these weather patterns as well as they do. I learned them from up here on the bridge."

Carson looked directly at the captain. "And you don't want to change course?"

Einer Sarninen slammed a fist to the chart-table top. His blocky face was purpling. "I do not!" he shouted. He clumped across the chart room and went out to the bridge wing, then below to his in-port cabin.

"I'll relieve you now, Mr. Mate," Mako said.

Midmorning, Sarninen climbed to the bridge again and looked at the graying expanse ahead. "Any traffic?" he asked.

"Nothing near, sir," Mako replied.

"All right. Put her on automatic pilot and let the

helmsman stand lookout. I want to talk to you.''

Mako took a deep breath and made the adjustment to automatic pilot, stationed the lookout, and followed Sarninen down the ladder.

At the open door, the captain halted. Inside, Mako could see Cajun standing at the captain's desk. The top drawer was open.

Sarninen snapped, "What are you doing at my desk?"

Cajun turned, suddenly pale. Sarninen stepped inside, and Mako followed. The messboy cleaned the cabin every morning, made the bed. As Mako neared the desk, he could see a revolver in the open drawer.

"All right, what were you doing?"

"Jus' cleaning, Cap'n."

"Don't ever open that drawer again," Sarninen roared.

Cajun nodded and moved to another corner of the room, plying a mop.

In the few minutes Mako had spent in the cabin on boarding the ship, he hadn't paid any attention to the titles of the books in the captain's case. Now he saw they were indeed mostly classics.

Sarninen seated himself. Mako glanced over at Cajun. "He can hear what I've got to say to you. He's involved."

An officer should never be reprimanded in front of the crew, Mako knew.

"I'm sorry I can't offer you a chair, Mr. Mako." There was an empty chair just a few feet away.

"That's quite all right, sir."

"Actually, I'm not sorry at all to have you stand. I really deserve that much respect."

Mako remained silent. He stood erect, balancing with the movement of the ship.

"Don't you agree?"

"Yes, sir, I agree."

The *Morning Light's* master suddenly smiled. "I was certain you would; you're a gentleman."

"I try to be."

"And you also acknowledge that you were wrong to countermand my order concerning this boy over here."

"I apologized yesterday, sir."

Sarninen slapped the arms of his chair. "Time for my inspection of the ship, and time for you to go back on watch. We'll talk again, many times. And if you ever want to read . . ." Sarninen waved toward his bookshelves. "I've got the best library in the tanker fleet. Not cheap, trashy paperbacks. You ever read *Walden*?"

"Yes, sir, quite a while ago," Mako said.

Mako almost reached the door when Sarninen spoke again. "Ever been in a hurricane, Mr. Mako?"

"No, Cap'n, I have not." Mako turned back toward Sarninen. He noticed that Cajun had stopped sweeping and was listening intently, staring at the captain. He also felt that what Sarninen said was for Cajun's ears, not his.

The captain glanced at the messboy. "You ever been in one, Cajun?"

Cajun nodded and held up a single finger.

"Then you know that the sea becomes wild."

Cajun swallowed. "We're goin' into it, Cap'n?"

Sarninen nodded. "Take you as close as I can without breaking the dishes." Smiling, he continued, "We'll call it Cajun's storm. Miami names them, why can't we? Mr. Mako, when those hurricane warnings come in, change the name from Babs to Cajun. We got a celebrity aboard.''

''Can't we go back?'' Cajun said, fear written all over his potato face.

Sarninen laughed heartily. ''No, Cajun.''

''May I be excused, Cap'n?'' Mako said.

''What's keeping you, Third?'' Sarninen replied.

In the wheelhouse, Mako returned the control to manual and put the helmsman back on wheel watch. The skies ahead were thickening and squall lines were beginning to form. Mako pulled a slicker out of the bridge locker and went to the wing to pass the rest of the morning, spray and freshening wind bathing his face.

His dad had wanted him to go to medical school and his mother had thought that Yale and a lawyer's life would be just fine. Jack had opted for the sea because he loved it. He'd built his own rowboat before he was ten, bought a sailboat when he was fourteen, entered the Merchant Marine Academy when he was eighteen. If he'd had a choice, he would have picked another ship, another captain, to start his career; but he was where he wanted to be, out on the water, despite Babs.

Fusari took the bridge watch at noon but they exchanged few words.

Mako ate with Stern. The captain was having lunch in his in-port cabin and Rodney had turned in for a nap.

The old engineer was in a talkative mood and Mako asked, ''How long have you been with the captain?''

''We came on this ship together ten years ago but I've known him for thirty.''

Choosing his words carefully, Mako said, "He's not an easy man to understand."

Stern looked down at his Spanish rice contemplatively and then raised the white mane again. "Mako, during the war with the Nazis, Sarninen was master of a tanker that got it off Cape Hatteras. Dead o' winter. He ended up in a lifeboat with ten other men. A navy destroyer came alongside and was ready to throw them a line when they got a sub contact. The destroyer took off after the sub and never came back. A week later, that lifeboat drifted ashore at Cape Henlopen. There were eleven frozen men in it but one was alive. Sarninen. Too tough to die." Stern snorted reflectively. "At least, that's what Einer told himself."

Mako heard him out and then said evenly, "That's not enough for the way he treats people. Cajun, for example."

"No other skipper'd take Cajun, be my guess. Sarninen's been good to him, in his own way, putting up with that drunkenness for the last three years."

The *Morning Light* took its first heavy roller and shivered all the way back to the fantail. The plates on the mess table hopped with vibration.

"That's a forecast," Stern murmured, cocking his ear to listen to the sea.

Cajun came out of the galley, face white with fear. "Is that the hurricane, Chief?" he asked.

"Not yet."

"My training said to stay away from them, if possible," Mako offered. "Carson thinks so, too."

"I have to tell you about tankers, young man. We're loaded down to the marks. The seas will just roll over us. We're better off loaded than light. If we had no cargo, the captain would pump ballast in until we were heavy. The only thing I worry about is that old wound when her back was broken. And so far as Carson is concerned, he'll never see the day when he knows the water like Einer Sarninen.''

Mako finished the meal without further conversation.

Midafternoon, when the SS *Morning Light* was beginning to slug at the building seas, Mako was sprawled out on his bunk, reading. There was a knock on the door and he said, ''Come in.''

The door opened slowly, and Cajun stood there timidly. ''Can Ah get you somethin', Mate?''

Mako raised himself up on his elbows. ''No thanks, Cajun.''

The messman scuffed his feet. ''Mate, Ah'd like to thank you again for what you did de other night. I mean wit' de water . . .''

Mako smiled. ''That's OK. Come on in and sit down.''

Cajun eased himself in and sat gingerly at Mako's small desk. His tongue dug around under his lips and Mako noticed he was wringing his hands. ''Mate, Ah'm scairt to death 'bout dat storm,'' he finally blurted.

''There's nothing much to be worried about, Cajun,'' Mako lied comfortingly. ''This old ship's been through a lot of storms.''

''You heard what de cap'n said, an' you heard what Rodney said 'bout it twistin' us in half . . .''

''Cajun, don't pay any attention to what they're saying.''

Cajun nodded and then, without a word, got up and left the room.

Mako tried to rekindle interest in the paperback, but Sarninen and the hurricane occupied his mind, and he gave it up after a few minutes to write several letters. The ship had begun to creak and he paused several times just to listen. Just after five, he went up to the bridge to read the latest Miami advisory and relieve Carson for his dinner.

Carson was at a forward port, staring into the muck. Rain squalls were ahead. "Any change?" Mako asked.

Carson shook his head. "We still haven't hit the edge. This stuff is outer fringe."

Mako went on into the chart room. The Miami report still indicated intensifying winds and now predicted they might reach 120 miles an hour. The hurricane hunters had again penetrated Babs at noon. Puerto Rico, the Dominican Republic, Cuba, and Haiti were all on alert. Florida had been added during the morning.

It took raw guts to fly those twin-engined P_2V Neptunes into the heart of the storm. Mako could imagine the beating the air crews took. He heard they sometimes vomited from fear of the wings being wrenched off or losing an engine. Riding it out on the surface of the sea was much, much better.

Carson left him guarding these thoughts and went aft to the officer's mess and dinner.

Thirty minutes later the chief mate relieved Mako with word that tonight's meal was vegetable soup, pork loin, and pasta, with apple pie for dessert. Tankers always served better food than freighters.

During his meal, Mako noticed that Cajun was almost helpless. He spilled food, his hands fluttering uncontrollably. Sarninen once again took pleasure in reminding the messman of the violent night ahead.

He built up a word picture of green seas that might carry the superstructure away, and by meal's end he had reduced Cajun to incoherency.

Mako picked at his food angrily while listening to the captain bait the messman. Then the master of the *Morning Light* rose, patted his stomach, and told Cajun to compliment the cook for such a fine meal on a lousy night. He departed for the bridge.

Stern tried to salvage Sarninen's wreckage. "Cajun," he said, "the old man was pulling your leg. We're not going to get into much of it." But Stern, himself, was not very convincing.

At seven-thirty, Mako again returned to the mess for a bracing cup of coffee before taking over the watch. Rodney was there, doing the same. Pots and pans were rattling in the galley, and the glasses in their wooden racks set up an eerie tympany.

Rodney was tired and oil stained, after having worked a full afternoon. He shouted to Cajun, "Better keep that coffee coming. We got a pump breakdown, as usual."

"Anything serious?" Mako asked.

"Not as long as the rest hold up."

Cajun entered with fresh coffee. "Yuh can fix it, can't yuh, Mr. Rodney?"

Rodney laughed. "Maybe. A little baling wire and pliers. That's what this ship is held together with." Then he asked Mako, "How's that great captain of ours doing?"

Mako shrugged. "He's up on the bridge, where he should be."

"I'll bet you a night out in Philly that he goes to bed just to show the rest of us he has guts."

"I won't take your bet, Rodney."

Rodney dropped his spoon with an angry clatter. "He must think he's got an angel perched on his shoulder. He ought to come down to the engine room. He'd change his mind."

Cajun was still listening and Mako wished that Rodney would shut up.

There was a sharp buzz on the communication panel. The bridge sign lit up. Cajun flipped a button and the buzzing ceased.

"De chief mate want his hot milk," Cajun said.

"His hot milk!" Rodney exploded.

Mako laughed. "I might try some."

Rodney said suddenly, "You ever seen an old hull come apart? Rivets fly like bees out of a hive. Hot milk?"

Mako was silent, watching Cajun.

"Ship's like a human being. Break a bone and it never heals as solid as before." He got up. "Keep that coffee hot, Cajun."

The door opened and cold spray drove in. Then Rodney vanished into the night. Mako pulled on his raincoat and headed for the bridge.

As he entered the wheelhouse, he made out the forms of Sarninen and Carson standing by the bridge ports. The gyrocompass clicked softly as the helmsman sought to compensate the swinging needle. They turned and looked at Mako.

"I think I'll get a few hours of sleep," Sarninen said.

Rodney had been right, Mako thought. "Any instructions, Cap'n?"

"Just wake me if you can't handle it. It'll do you good to stand a watch alone on a night like this. Schoolie education."

Mako watched as the Finn moved toward the chart room, then toward his sea cabin.

"You want me to stand it with you?" Carson asked. Mako was reminded again that this was his first voyage as an officer, first encounter with a major hurricane.

"No, I'll be OK."

With a lash of wind and rain, Cox opened the outer door to relieve the helm. Carson rubbed his eyes. It was a strain to look at the white turbulence and he'd been on watch four hours.

"Any instructions for me?" Mako asked.

Carson looked over and said quietly, "Just wake the skipper if she starts to break up." The big mate moved toward the chart room door and the stair exit to the cabins below. "By the way, wake me, too."

Mako turned again to the port to see the bow eat fifty tons of water with every hillock of dark sea. Behind him, he heard Cox relieving.

"Steer oh-one-oh, she's falling off to the left," said Carson's helmsman.

Cox repeated the heading and then murmured, "I got her," and Jack Mako's watch settled down until midnight.

The SS *Morning Light* plunged and bucked along. His ears attuned to the ship's noises now, and his body automatically reflexing to the rise and fall, Mako began to relax a little. Perhaps Sarninen was right. She could ride out a good blow.

Sometime after ten, Cajun appeared from the chart room with a tray of hot coffee. Mako marveled that the messman had made it across the heaving catwalk. Cajun wore a torn slicker, and water was streaming down his face. He put the tray down on a bridge rail shelf and Mako poured a cup.

"Gettin' worse?" Cajun asked.

"About the same."

There was a heavy, booming noise and the wheel-house shook violently. Mako stepped back to his port, thinking he should call the engine room and reduce propeller revolutions. He knew he should awaken the captain first, but declined that move. He said to Cajun, "See, she took a good one then, but you notice how she shook it off." He looked at Cajun closely. The terror was still there.

Cajun's tongue flicked around his dry lips. "If anything happens tonight, Mate, jus' remember Ah 'preciate what you done for me."

Mako frowned at the little man. "Forget it, Cajun. Just stay off the bottle when we get to Philadelphia."

Cajun lingered a moment longer, looking at the third, then slipped away.

The *Morning Light* dug in again, and Mako watched a sheet of white water, jagged and wind-caught, mount into the air almost to the crow's nest.

Mako yelled to Cox, "You gotta keep that bow on!"

"I'm tryin' . . ."

One solution was to reduce speed, cut down on those propeller revolutions.

The bridge phone rang. It was Stern wanting the captain.

Mako said, "He's in the sea cabin," and heard the phone bang down. He stepped back to the sea cabin and peered inside.

Sarninen was fully dressed. Sound asleep. His body rolled easily and unconcernedly with the movement of the ship. The phone rang and Sarninen reached for it in an action so wide-awake and swift that Mako's eyes could not cover it.

"Yes," he barked.

Stern's voice was filtered but loud. "Cap'n, we can't fix the emergency fuel pump."

"The main pump's all right, isn't it?"

"Right now, but we had trouble with it coming down here. Remember?"

"You tryin' to invent an excuse and make me turn around, Joe?"

Mako heard Stern's angry reply: "Einer, you know better than that! I don't invent excuses. I've informed you of a pump breakdown. If you don't want to do anything about it, that's your business."

Sarninen roared into the phone, "I don't want to do anything about it." He hung up and then saw Mako. "Well, what do *you* want?"

"I think we should reduce revolutions, Cap'n. She's pounding."

Sarninen swung his feet over the side of his bed to put his shoes on. "I can hear, Mr. Mako. I can also feel. I know she's pounding."

Mako nodded a "Yes, sir" and returned to the wheelhouse.

In a moment, he was joined by the captain. "You get some sleep, sir?" It was obvious he had. Untroubled, miraculous sleep. Mako felt like slugging him.

Sarninen merely grunted. Then stared out ahead. "Well, you've kept her afloat, Mr. Mako. She isn't quite the derelict that Rodney and others would have you think." He watched the bow with a practiced eye for a moment, then said, "Call the engineers and have them take ten revs off."

Soon, the *Morning Light* rode easier, and Mako was thankfully relieved at midnight by Fusari. But she was still quivering stem to stern with every sea, and Hurricane Babs was coming closer.

As he was getting into his bunk, Mako heard a voice in the passageway. It sounded like Cajun's. He stepped outside and saw the messman standing in Carson's doorway. Mako took a few steps forward and gasped as he saw a pistol in Cajun's right hand. He heard Carson ask, "Cajun, what's wrong with you?"

And he heard Cajun answer, "Ah'll kill you, Mr. Carson, 'less the cap'n turns dis ship around."

Mako placed his back against the steel bulkhead of the passageway and edged toward Carson's door. Cajun had gone inside the cabin and was holding the pistol a few inches from the chief mate's temple. Carson was sitting in his desk chair, clad in his underwear.

His voice was calm but his face was white with fear. He said, "Cajun, we're not in any danger. Honest! Put the gun down and let's go up and talk to the captain."

"Wouldn't do no good, Mate, but if the captain knows somethin' will happen to you, he'll turn around . . ."

Carson shook his head. "He won't turn around for me."

Carson moved slightly in his chair. The way he was facing, Mako knew Cajun couldn't see him. But Cajun was in such a position that Mako couldn't reach him without the gun going off.

Carson suddenly began to plead. The ship was plunging and bucking, and the roar of water outside could be heard in the passageway and by Cajun.

"Cajun, you can't stand there all night and I can't sit here . . ." Dry-mouthed fear was in Carson's voice.

Mako was now directly across from the doorway and he forced himself to sound natural, as if he were ordering a steak back in officer's mess. "Cajun, what are you doing?"

Cajun turned his head slightly to glimpse the third mate. "Tell the cap'n Ah'm gonna kill Mr. Carson 'less he turns the ship aroun' right now."

"Believe me, Cajun, we're not in danger."

Cajun shook his head obstinately. "Storm's gonna twiss us in half . . ."

Carson said, "It's no use, Mako. You better tell the old man."

Mako lingered in the passageway as Carson began to talk soothingly to Cajun. "See that picture on my desk here? That's my wife . . . and family . . . two boys. Now, you wouldn't want to hurt them . . ."

As Mako edged away, he could hear Carson droning on. He ran up the inside steps to the wheelhouse and through the chart room. "Cap'n, Cajun's got a gun on the first mate."

Sarninen and Fusari simultaneously swung their heads, then Sarninen laughed wildly. "Is it loaded with bourbon?"

Mako shouted back, "He's got a gun, Cap'n Sarninen! Probably yours. He's going to kill Carson if you don't turn this ship around."

Sarninen's eyes narrowed. "What is this? Some kind of plot you and Cajun cooked up to make me change course?"

"For God's sake, Cap'n," Mako raged. "Please listen to me. Cajun is scared out of his mind."

"He's always been crazy," Sarninen yelled. "Don't you know that?"

Mako lowered his voice. "You better come down, Cap'n."

"Don't tell me what to do, Mako. Go tell Cajun to give you that gun, or I'll personally throw him over the side tonight. He can get a real mouthful of storm."

"Sir, that's not going to scare him. He's off, clear off . . ."

Sarninen glared at Mako for a moment, then said, "Come with me."

Mako followed him into the chart room.

The captain bent down at the small safe, once used for secret convoy instructions during the war, and moved the dial back and forth until it opened. He extracted a .38-caliber pistol, passing it toward Mako. "It's my extra one for times like this. Now go down and get that gun from Cajun."

Mako stared at the pistol. "He's your monster, Captain Sarninen. You created him. You bullied him, you goaded him, you scared him . . ."

"Mr. Mako, I gave you an order," Sarninen roared.

"I refuse."

Sarninen sneered, "You mean, Mr. Mako, that you can't take a gun away from a feebleminded messboy?"

"I mean you are going to have a murder on your hands unless you turn the ship around."

Sarninen became livid as he moved back toward the wheelhouse. "I'm not changing course for Cajun, Carson, you, or anyone else." He turned back. "Take this gun and do as I ordered. Shoot him if he doesn't obey."

Mako felt exhausted. "He'll pull the trigger unless I tell him you've agreed."

"I'm giving you an order—" and he smashed the gun into Mako's hand. "Witness this, Mr. Fusari,

I'm giving this officer an order. You'll testify before the Coast Guard.''

Mako stared at the captain with defiance. ''You don't have the right to give that kind of order,'' and passed the pistol back to the master of the *Morning Light*.

Sarninen said to Fusari, ''Take the bridge. I'm going below.'' He brushed past the third without a word.

Mako descended the steps. No man had the right to ask what Sarninen had asked. Not even at sea, not even the master. No mate could be ordered to use a gun, to risk his life that way, especially when the master himself was responsible for a crewman's terror.

The captain's footsteps pounded down the steel deck of the passageway, then Mako heard Sarninen's deadly voice, ''Ca-j-u-n-n, give me that gun. You don't know what you're doing. That gun, Cajun . . .'' The captain was standing outside Carson's cabin doorway.

Mako stopped and gasped at the sudden explosion, then ran the twenty feet as Sarninen's back slowly slid down the bulkhead, his knees buckling. Mako caught him just before he hit the deck. There was stunned surprise on his face.

Sarninen knew it was Mako by his side; he murmured, ''Never . . . refuse . . . an order . . . Mako.'' Then his head slumped and blood trickled from his lips.

Mako looked around. Carson was pushing up from his desk. Cajun's eyes were wide, his face a blank.

Carson took the gun from Cajun's hand, then moved into the passageway to bend over Sarninen.

"Help me get him to the bunk." They carried him inside Carson's cabin.

Cajun was standing just inside the doorway. The torment had left him. Tears were streaming down the potato face. Carson told him to return aft, and he began cutting the captain's bloodstained shirt away.

The bullet, which Mako knew could have been in his own body, had left a hole in Sarninen's chest. Carson said, "Looks bad. Have Sparks call the Coast Guard and ask them for medical advice." Sparks was the radioman.

Mako, now feeling overwhelming guilt, hurried off. When he returned, Chief Stern was in the cabin. He read Mako's mind. He said, "Cajun just shot the best friend he's ever had."

Was Stern crazy? Mako thought.

"They understood each other. Nothing is all love or hate. Life is a learning experience. You just learned another lesson," Stern said, and pulled a chair up beside Sarninen. The captain's breathing was labored but he was still alive.

Mako followed Carson up to the bridge. The chief mate said quietly to Fusari, "Cajun shot the skipper. He may not live. Let's come about. We'll head due west for the next twelve hours. We'll run from Babs."

The *Morning Light* began to fall off and then wallowed through the turn.

Mako said, with anguish, "He ordered me to go down there with the gun. I refused."

Carson didn't answer.

"It was Sarninen who drove Cajun out of his mind, no matter what the chief engineer said."

The big mate said, "Yes, I know."

"What will happen to Cajun?"

"Depends on whether or not the skipper dies. Either way, he has a problem."

Mako took a deep breath. "What will happen to me?"

"There'll be a hearing about all of this, and it'll include Cajun, and you, and me, and the skipper, dead or alive. We all make mistakes. To tell you truthfully, I'd thought about forcing the skipper to turn southwest yesterday, one way or another. I was as scared as Cajun that we'd break up."

Mako went out on the bridge wing and let the savage wind and spray attack his face. He looked into the stormswept night and listened to the hostile growl of the wind.

No matter what happened at the hearing on this first and perhaps last voyage as a third mate, he knew that for as long as he lived he'd hear, *Never . . . refuse . . . an order . . . Mako.*

He shouted into the wind, "God, don't let him die . . ."

The 6:00 A.M. advisory from the Hurricane Center in Miami said that Babs had sharply changed course and would now go up Mona Passage, between the Dominican Republic and Puerto Rico. Captain Sarninen had been right after all.

Chief Mate Carson told Mako, "Have the helmsman put her back on her old course. We'll proceed directly to Philadelphia." They'd go through Windward Passage, west of Haiti, as Einer Sarninen had so carefully plotted.

The "O Tannenbaum" Affair

*E*ven now, when 99.9 percent of all the old secrets have been told, those cagey fellows in U.S. Naval Intelligence still deny that an outfit called QA, Question and Answer, ever existed during the big war—World War II, the one before Korea or Vietnam or Desert Storm. But the Office of Naval Intelligence–QA existed, all right, and for one purpose only: to get information from surviving German U-boat sailors, by fair means or foul. In 1942 the seas were littered with debris, and American beaches were coated with black oil scum from sunken Allied ships. For ten months ONI–QA didn't even justify a clip on the piece of paper that caused it to be organized, but then . . .

Five nights before Christmas 1942, a navy C-47 transport landed at the Norfolk Naval Air Station, taxied up to within a hundred yards of the Operations Building canopy, and cut its engines.

An overcoated British naval lieutenant, temporarily attached to QA, emerged from the aircraft door and stood for a moment at the top of the steps, looking over the dark, deserted field. The last antisubmarine patrols had taken off at midnight, their exhaust stacks spitting blue flame on a northerly course, and the field was secured until dawn.

For a moment the lieutenant seemed uncertain what to do next. He scanned the dimly lit Operations Building, shrugged, and, carrying a small flight bag and a large briefcase, descended from the plane, followed by five American yeomen, navy clerk-typists.

He moved his tall, skinny frame a few paces and then deposited the hand luggage on the ground, as if awaiting someone.

One of the sailors approached him. "Sir, was there another officer supposed to be on that plane?"

"I really don't know," the lieutenant replied, in as polished a British accent as could be found anywhere in the Isles.

The sailor was short, tending to pudginess, blue eyed, and blond, with wire-rimmed spectacles and a baby face. He said, "I'm Otto Kesler, yeoman first class, and I'm looking for Lieutenant Clay Shuford. I thought he'd be on that flight." He glanced back toward the darkened aircraft.

"I'm Clay Shuford, Royal Navy Reserve," said the lieutenant.

Kesler was stunned. "But you're British . . ."

Shuford looked amused. "Yes, I apologize." Funny how this was occurring on both sides of the Atlantic. When an American showed up in a British unit, it was invariably, "Whot, a Yank?"

Kesler laughed weakly. "I just didn't expect a British officer. Why, I sat across from you all the way from Washington." Then he peered closely at Shuford. "You're intelligence, too."

"I'm afraid so, temporarily attached to your American ONI."

Kesler turned to the other men, waving his head toward Shuford. "This is the lieutenant," he said. Then he turned back to Shuford as they came closer. "We're your yeomen, sir. Schroder, Goldberg, Honig, Geiger, and myself."

The men nodded a greeting.

Shuford looked too old to be only a lieutenant, Otto Kesler thought. He must have been at least forty, maybe older. Kesler had glanced at Shuford on the plane, noted the gray thinning hair and the black eye patch. The face was finely drawn, almost poetic, and the brow was intellectual. If he'd ever been in sunlight, other than what came through a window, it didn't show. Shuford looked more like a college professor than a naval officer.

"Sir, what's this all about?" Goldberg asked. "They dumped me out of my bunk three hours ago and told me to sit my haunch in a bucket seat for a midnight ride to Norfolk." Their orders had been, "Report immediately to ONI Staff, Norfolk Naval Operating Base, for temporary duty." They hadn't been told more.

Shuford surveyed them. They were young—nineteen, maybe twenty at the oldest—a bright-looking lot, bundled in their peacoats against the cold air that was slicing off Hampton Roads. Honig looked like a juvenile con man. Schroder was absolutely German, or appeared that way. Goldberg's face was a pale moon. Hans Geiger and Otto Kesler looked as Anglo-Saxon as Yorkshire pudding by way of Philadelphia; but, like the others, they'd been born of German parents and had spoken the language at home. Shuford had been hurriedly briefed about them.

"You're all stationed in Washington," he said.

"Yes, sir. Intelligence yeoman pool," Kesler answered.

Shuford nodded. "Well, I really don't know much more than you do. I was called at eleven o'clock. I do know that one of your destroyers got a Nazi sub off Cape Hatteras at dusk last night. Fine piece of work, I'd say. An early gift from your Santa Claus. Three survivors, including the skipper. Our targets now."

"So they finally got one, eh? Some gift," Kesler murmured in pleased surprise.

"Rather looks that way, and rather looks as if that's why we're here." Shuford studied the yeomen and addressed Kesler. "First, I've been told that all of you understand and speak German fluently?"

Kesler replied quickly and proudly, "Yes, sir. Speak it, write it, read it, and understand it. And there's a difference in that last one."

"Good. Very good," Shuford said approvingly. Then, looking from young face to young face, he said, "I realize you'd rather be home with your loved ones this season, and I promise I'll try to get you there by Christmas Eve."

"Appreciate that, sir," said Kesler. He wasn't exactly happy about this new duty. He didn't want to miss Christmas at home in Philadelphia with his girlfriend and family. The others, excepting Goldberg, felt the same, he knew. Christmas was always special in German Protestant families, and no one knew where they'd be next year.

"I do understand," said Shuford, glancing toward the Operations Building. "Well, since there's no welcome party at two A.M., let's make it on our own."

Shuford walked rapidly ahead and Kesler hurried to catch up with him, as did the others.

"I assume you've heard of Captain Haines, the ONI commander here," Shuford said.

"Yes, sir. My chief told me he's a tough one. He's sweating out this miserable job until he gets a division of submarines in the Pacific. He's chompin' at the bit."

Shuford frowned. "Chompin' at the bit?"

Kesler nodded. "My chief told me he's not an intelligence man. He hates the cloak-and-dagger routine. Big ex-football player at the Naval Academy. Cap'n Haines is a fighting man, and a war doesn't come along every year, my chief said."

Shuford raised his eyebrows and said in a soft voice, "Thank God."

They continued under the canopy into Operations, Kesler and his group going on to Enlisted Personnel to check in.

At six in the foggy morning, Lieutenant Shuford and Captain Arthur Haines, USN, were on a pier in the naval operating base. Dock lights were still on and they cast shadows along the superstructures of several harbor craft. Haines's car, a gray navy sedan, and a panel-type truck from the Shore Patrol with a heavily armed sailor leaning against the fender were parked a few yards away.

Haines, a bluff, ruddy-faced man, his thick neck encased in a white silk scarf, gazed out sleepily from beneath his scrambled-egg hat brim toward the dark, chopping water of Hampton Roads, the great harbor just inside the meeting point of Chesapeake Bay and the Atlantic Ocean.

Shuford estimated him to be about fifty years old, and also estimated him to be suffering from something besides dawn surliness. Perhaps Kesler was right. The captain saw a grand war—and a chance to become an admiral—slipping past his trigger finger. Haines had done nothing more than offer a series of granite-y grunts when they'd met twenty minutes before.

In the near distance, the jerky cough of a diesel engine advised them that the navy tug was rounding the pier head. After a moment it stuck its stubby, buffered prow into view, moving slowly toward the dock.

Shivering, Shuford said, "They're taking their bloody good time in this cold."

"You should be right at home in this weather, Lieutenant," said Haines. "We brought it to the Virginia capes just for you. Perfect British weather, which means lousy."

Shuford ignored the dig and said, more to himself, "Cuts to the marrow, this cold. They must be paddling that craft."

"It's a tugboat, Mr. Shuford. Not a speedboat." Haines checked his watch. "And if you know *anything* about the sea, he's averaged ten knots since he left Hatteras last night. I don't think His Majesty's Navy could have done better under the circumstances."

Shuford agreed with a respectful nod, and then Haines turned slightly to speak to the sailor police behind them. Two more had joined the SP leaning on the fender. "Take the prisoners directly to Sick Bay as soon as we get them on the dock. I understand they're covered with oil. I've called the medical officer on watch to be ready for them.''

The senior of the burly SP's responded, ''Yes, sir, Cap'n Haines,'' as the sharp, quick blasts of the tug's whistle stabbed the lifting dark. Then she bumped alongside.

A door on the starboard side popped open and three men wrapped in blankets emerged. Stepping out behind them in foul-weather gear was a sailor, machine gun cradled in his arm. It occurred to Shuford that these might be the most important prisoners of war that the navy had ever taken.

The three men, faces and hair coated with gummy oil, stared up at the dock in hostility, and Haines joined Shuford in an equally hostile stare toward the tug's deck.

''I'd wager the one in the middle is Hedmann,'' Shuford muttered. ''Observe the proud carriage and the arrogance.''

''We'll break that arrogance,'' Haines replied.

The man in the middle, if Shuford's assumption was correct, was *Kapitänleutnant* Horst Hedmann, former commanding officer of the U-boat. From prior intelligence information hurriedly gathered, they knew that he was in his middle thirties and had patrolled at least once—and very successfully— along the mid-Atlantic lanes. He was stocky and— even with the thick coating of oil—a handsome, defiant man. His eyes burned from his blackened face like twin nubs of smoldering punk.

The tug was barely secured when the sailor with the machine gun unceremoniously prodded the prisoners up the ladder toward the group on the dock. In a moment they were facing Captain Haines and Lieutenant Shuford.

Shuford said courteously, speaking to them all, *"Guten Morgen, meine Herren. Sprechen Sie Englisch?"* Good morning, gentlemen. Do you speak English?

They stood dumbly, but Shuford noticed that the one to the left of the man he assumed to be *Kapitän* Hedmann glanced about nervously, as if awaiting a signal from his commanding officer. Then the stocky man in the center said, with dignity, "Under the Geneva Convention, I am only required to give you our names, ranks, and serial numbers." He paused and glanced at the flossy scrambled eggs on Haines's hat. "I do speak adequate English, and my further answer to you is, 'Good morning, gentlemen. Do you speak German?' "

Shuford smiled. "I try," he said pleasantly. "What are your names?"

"Kapitänleutnant Horst Hedmann."

Shuford nodded. He'd guessed right.

The others did not speak, and Hedmann identified them. "Heinrich Bauer, my second officer." The man to his right stiffened a bit. He was small and wiry, with dark, curly hair. He appeared to be in his early twenties.

"Schlisser, torpedoman, third." The man on Hedmann's left wiped his smudged face nervously, and the eyes of the U-boat commander narrowed.

Shuford nodded again and made a quick guess that Hedmann was wishing this man hadn't survived. Schlisser was obviously of peasant stock. About eighteen, Shuford guessed. His hair had been cut with a bowl.

Hedmann continued, "We are the only survivors. Two men died in my arms in the water. Your destroyer did a very good job."

"A very good job at last," Captain Haines re-torted coldly. "But too late to save that tanker. I'm curious to know—"

Hedmann's eyes came quickly to the captain. "Whatever you're curious to know, Captain, I doubt you will ever find out. Meanwhile my men have had a severe night, and it is cold out here."

Captain Haines's eyes were as frigid as the water that lapped the dock beside them. He glared at Hedmann for a moment and then turned again to the SP's. "All right, take them to Sick Bay, turn them over to the doctor, and have them fed. They can sleep awhile."

The burly lead sailor saluted and almost with the same motion used the end of his machine gun to direct the Germans to the panel truck. Watching them go, Shuford said to Haines, "You have your work cut out for you, Captain."

"No, *you* do," Haines corrected with a swift glance. "Washington must have thought I needed help down here. They sent a junior officer of a foreign navy. But you should know I didn't request your help, Lieutenant."

Shuford remained silent. There was really no answer. He was on the Royal Navy promotion list but the extra rank hadn't come through as yet. He *was* an aging junior officer.

They heard Hedmann's voice again: "Sirs!" He was about to step into the panel truck. Bauer and Schlisser were already inside. Hedmann loosened the blanket around his shoulders and drew himself proudly erect. He said, "I apologize for my tone of voice, Captain. I am sure you understand I am suf-fering from the disgrace of being the first German submarine commander to be taken alive in American waters."

With that he moved, almost nobly, inside; and then the truck backed slowly off the dock.

In a security area well away from the docks and the airfield, a one-story wooden building that was designated ONI stood inside a steel-wire fence twelve feet high. There were two entrances to it and guards now stood twenty-four hours a day at these. At night the grounds around the building were brilliantly lighted, and every bush had been removed; even the crawlspaces beneath the building had been cemented. There was still the usual flagpole, though; here, each sunrise, the flag was hauled up; and here, each night, the flag came down. The bugler, not an ONI person, blew taps just as he had before December 7 of the past year, when this had been a regular part of the base.

The yeomen had been assigned their bunkroom spaces in the ONI compound and were unpacking. The building was of a long, low barracks type divided into two wings. The yeomen were in the south wing, alongside the temporary office and living spaces of Captain Haines and his staff, and Lieutenant Shuford. The prisoners would be in the north wing.

Honig finished his unpacking first and said with a sigh, "We're going to be working with that Limey looie every day? Big deal."

"He's an expert," Kesler answered. "The Brits have been fighting the Germans for a long time. They know the enemy better than we do. I'll make a bet that Shuford has some surprises for that sub commander."

*   *   *

In Sick Bay, the prisoners sat stripped, except for towels across their loins, while medical corpsmen sponged oil from their bodies. Nearby, on the surgical tables, were piles of stained clothing. The prisoners sat silent and expressionless.

The teenaged corpsman who was repairing Schlisser tossed his sponge into a bucket of gasoline and said cheerfully, "All done. You want some coffee?"

Schlisser understood "coffee" but was uncertain about accepting the cup. He glanced at Hedmann. The commanding officer nodded approval.

The corpsman, seeing the exchange, laughed. "Got no poison in it."

"*Danke, danke,*" Schlisser replied. *Thank you, thank you.*

The corpsman looked at his fellow medical aides and shook his head. "I'll bet these guys have to raise their hands when they want to go to the head."

There was raucous laughter, but Hedmann stared straight ahead, his eyes the gray of the North Sea in the dead of winter.

In Haines's office, the captain, standing by a large area chart of the Atlantic, was saying, "They attacked the tanker here and hit it. And then the *Blevins* picked the U-boat up here, just south of Nag's Head." Haines tapped the chart. "Straddled him with depth charges in shallow water, forced him up, and then rammed him."

"What about salvage?" Shuford asked.

"We can't get to the hull. He managed to slide away into deeper water after he was rammed. Lucky devil."

Haines's office was small and very neat. There

were a few photographs of submarines on the walls, and Shuford assumed they were the captain's past commands. There was a washbasin and a medicine chest at one end of the room. The usual navy manuals were in a metal bookcase, on which was displayed, prominently, a football with white letters on it: ARMY–NAVY GAME—1929. On top of Haines's desk, at the front edge, was an elaborate carved wooden nameplate with big gold dolphin insignia trailing over each end. Crew's gift from one of his boats, very likely.

They moved away from the area chart and Haines took a seat behind his desk. Shuford leaned casually against it. Shuford noticed that Haines had a habit of rubbing the dolphin submariner emblem that was above his left breast pocket with his right thumb. But any man who wore that emblem had a right to be proud.

"Maneuvered away, huh?" Shuford resumed. "That indicates that Hedmann doesn't panic easily."

"Panic?" Haines scoffed. "The *Blevins* was just plain lucky. They've got some damnable device on those subs that lets them escape every time we make sound contact. Next thing we know, the gear is confused and they slip away."

"Our destroyers are worthless unless we find out what it is," Shuford mused.

Haines's face was unreadable in the halo of light from his desk lamp. "That's correct, Mr. Shuford."

Still thinking aloud, Shuford said, "Hedmann is suffering from disgrace. He admits it. All of them are tough and proud. None will trick easily."

"I agree," said Haines.

"I doubt Hedmann will ever crack. Perhaps the second officer, Bauer, will. Or maybe it would be best to concentrate on Schlisser, the enlisted man." With one long finger stroking slowly just beneath his ear, he added, "You're a submarine captain—"

"Tied to a desk," Haines interrupted sullenly.

"What would it take to get information out of you?"

A brittle laugh played out of Haines's thick lips. "To answer you honestly, Lieutenant, I don't think you're the type of man who could ever get information out of me. And to be perfectly honest again, Mr. Shuford, I don't see why they didn't send me down a combat man who understands the type."

Shuford frowned. "I didn't ask for this assignment, sir." He moved to the wall chart and stood viewing the sinking spot of the U-boat, marked with a red X. Then Shuford again faced the submariner. "Captain, life is full of surprises for us both," he said. "Three years ago I was in front of a classroom in Oxford. I taught languages. This morning, students of mine are likely fighting Rommel in the desert, or flying a Lancaster to Bremerhaven to bomb it. Better they should have gone to a weapons course. They don't need to converse with any enemy for what they're doing now."

Haines lowered his eyes for the first time. "Your point is well taken. I'm sure you have a place in the war."

"I'm a noncombatant because there is no eye here," Shuford continued coldly, tapping the black patch. "A childhood accident with a sweet stick."

Haines was suddenly annoyed. "Forget what I said about a combat man, and let's get on with the job."

"As you wish, sir," Shuford replied, restraining himself from giving an exaggerated salute.

Haines's face was blank in the oval of light. "How do you want it, Mr. Shuford?"

The lieutenant crossed again to stand in front of the dolphin nameplate. "I haven't had too much time to think, but going on past experience with Germans—in London, of course—I'd put Hedmann and Bauer in adjoining rooms, so they can chat. The rooms must be bugged, but whoever does it must make sure of concealment. Hedmann will surely examine every inch."

"I'll supervise it personally."

"I want the door to be unlocked between Hedmann's and Bauer's rooms, so there is freedom," Shuford continued. "The doors to the passageway must also be unlocked, but we'll put a guard outside each one."

Haines was intrigued. "That's quite a bit of freedom."

"I want the enlisted man, Schlisser, put in another room down the hall. Alone."

Haines began to scribble notes, swallowing the fact that the QA junior officer was in command this time.

"And the only contact with the prisoners will be from myself and the five German-speaking yeomen. I will forbid the guards to speak to the prisoners. And I'm sorry, Captain—that means you, too."

Haines glanced up, frowning, his jaw flexing, but he accepted the rules silently.

"I want them to have all the comforts. Anything they want. A radio. Newspapers. A bottle. Hedmann won't touch it, and Bauer may not—but I'd guess young Schlisser will. He'll want courage. Hedmann may order them not to touch it, for fear of loosening a tongue, but let's see what his reaction is."

Haines put the pencil down. "This is unorthodox, Mr. Shuford. Certainly a genteel way to treat prisoners."

"What would you do, Captain?" Shuford asked.

"I don't think I'd use your velvet methods. For the past six months I've seen bodies wash ashore on every tide. I've seen red glows at midnight from burning tankers." Haines rose from behind his desk, attempting to keep his mounting rage in control. "It isn't war along this coast, Mr. Shuford, it's U-boat slaughter.

"What would I do, Lieutenant? If it weren't for the Geneva Convention, I'd go into Sick Bay with a baseball bat—or better still, my bare hands. I'd beat the hell out of all three of them until they told me what it is that makes our destroyers useless."

Shuford's one good eye surveyed Captain Haines with complete detachment. "I wish it were that simple, Captain," he said quietly. "How I really wish it were that simple! Your method is the easiest, and in the end, the least painful."

Lieutenant Shuford departed, leaving the captain to examine his notes.

After breakfast Kesler was on his bunk, trying to sleep. He was desperately tired. Yet his mind kept on whirring with uncertainty. He'd made first less than two weeks ago and now had the responsibility for the performance of the others, who were snoring away.

He'd volunteered for navy service the day after he'd graduated from high school two years ago, and thought he'd be at sea after boot camp was finished. But then the Bureau of Personnel discovered he could speak and write German. He was quickly assigned to ONI. Trained as a clerk-typist in two months, he was rated up on mastering a stenotype machine. The others had similar experience but were still yeomen, second.

His section chief had called just before they left Washington last night, saying, "You guys better not blow this. A lot of people are dying out there and this is our big chance to stop it."

Kesler wasn't sure he was up to helping stop anything, much less U-boat torpedoes.

Shuford entered Sick Bay; a corpsman was posted at the reception desk, along with the burly SP. Standing nearby was a naval doctor in a white coat, signing a form. He was obviously the medical officer of the day.

"Where do I find the German prisoners, please?" Shuford asked.

"Down the passage," the corpsman said. "They're in rooms thirty-two and thirty-three, officer section, and forty-six, enlisted."

The doctor looked up. "No one is supposed to see them except ONI."

"I am ONI," Shuford replied.

"But you're British."

Shuford sighed. "That seems to be some kind of curse over here."

"They've been fed, but I'd recommend you let them get some sleep. They're exhausted."

"I have no intention of disturbing them. I simply want to ask the *Kapitänleutnant* one question, if he isn't dozing."

The doctor nodded reluctantly.

Shuford walked away and then, suddenly, turned back. "Doctor, are they all right?"

The doctor nodded again. "Physically, yes. Mentally, they're a little bruised."

"For my purpose, that is ideal. Thank you, Doctor," Shuford said, resuming his path down the slick linoleum.

The former commanding officer of the yet-to-be-identified U-boat was in bed but wide awake. Propped on his pillow, he angled his head over as Shuford entered. He had short-cropped blond hair and a strong jaw. He had a face of magnificent strength, and Shuford sensed that behind that Teutonic visage was a magnificent mind. It was a frightening prospect, because the combination of beauty and brilliance made him almost invulnerable. The only imaginable way to crack this man was to destroy his spirit.

Shuford smiled. "I won't keep you from sleep long."

The German did not return the smile.

"I simply want to ask you one question."

Hedmann gazed at the lieutenant and said, with deliberation, "You know I am not required to answer except for name, serial number, and rank. I will keep reminding you of that."

"I'm sure you will," Shuford said, the smile still warm and genuine on his thin cheeks. "My question is really quite trivial. I'd like to know in which part of Germany you grew up."

Hedmann frowned. "That is quite trivial, is it not?"

"Before the war I taught German at Oxford," Shuford continued. "I used to pride myself on being able to detect the home city of any of your countrymen simply by their inflection. Sort of a game. Now, I know you're not a Berliner . . . or Bavarian. I'd guess Hamburg, a man from the Alster.''

Hedmann regarded his opponent with interest. "But that isn't why you came in here," he said.

Shuford chuckled. "No. I simply wanted to see you with all that gunk wiped off.''

"What you see is very tired," Hedmann murmured, and slipped down on the pillow, turning to the wall. It was a signal for Shuford to leave.

"Danke, Kapitän. Später komme ich zurück." Shuford said gently. *Thank you, Captain. I'll see you later.*

The head on the pillow moved slightly at hearing the faultless German, but the back of it stayed resolutely toward Shuford. But then he heard a barely audible murmur: "Hamburg *is* my home. Over the weeks, I'd be interested in more of your guesses.''

From the Sick Bay Lieutenant Shuford walked to one of the entrances in the steel-wire fence surrounding the ONI barracks, displayed his ONI card, and proceeded to the barracks building. Although, for a number of reasons, it had not been committed to official records, the sole purpose of the barracks was as an interrogation center for the hapless *Kriegsmarine* U-boaters, survivors of subs like the one sunk off North Carolina.

Shuford located what would be Hedmann's room, with bath attached. It was furnished to his satisfaction, Shuford noted, with as much comfort as could be found in any senior naval officer's bachelor quarters. One large window overlooked the quadrangle. A lovely view for the *Kapitänleutnant*.

Captain Haines was in the room, overseeing two electricians. One electrician was on the high ladder while the other was passing up tools to him. "Try not to smudge the ceiling,'' Haines urged. ''He'll cover every inch of it.''

The electrician, a civilian, said, ''Do my best, sir.''

Haines, ignoring Shuford's presence, asked, ''How long do you think the other rooms will take?''

''We can finish them all by tonight,'' the civilian said.

Shuford glanced at the work being done to install the tiny microphone on the ceiling fixture, and frowned.

Haines caught the frown. He said, ''You'll also find two more, but I defy you to find the fourth one.''

Shuford moved around the room, scanning it, running his hands over every fixture. Then he came back to stand beside Captain Haines. He said, ''One in the ceiling, of course. One in that wall switch. Another in the heating unit . . .''

''You're very observant. Now, the fourth . . .''

Shuford shook his head.

Haines nodded upward. ''Inside the steam-line insulation. There'll be a hundred-ninety degrees in that pipe, and he can't touch it, even if he is suspicious.''

''Very clever,'' Shuford admitted, ''but not foolproof.''

''What is foolproof, Lieutenant?''

''Horst Hedmann may be very close to being foolproof. I just left him, and on the way back here from Sick Bay, it occurred to me that any success we may have with his interrogation will be entirely accidental—and then it will be up to us to take advantage of the accident.''

The lieutenant's negativism was beginning to irritate Haines. ''My telephone orders from Washington were to let you handle the job under my loose supervision. I expect I'm supposed to learn something from you and this cockeyed Question-Answer unit you're with, but unless I have some results to report within forty-eight hours, that supervision is going to become extremely tight and uncomfortable for you."

Shuford held his ground. "The baseball bat, sir?"

"Let's say the direct approach, my remedy for most things," Haines replied grimly.

Shuford sighed deeply; he did not know how to cope with Haines. Then he nodded. "Would you excuse me, sir? I have a little homework to do. The antisubmarine warfare section gave me a complete dossier on the U-85 type and I haven't had a chance to study it. I'm guessing the boat was a U-85 type."

Haines looked at the British officer. "Yes, you could do with a little study about submarines. You're dismissed, Mr. Shuford."

That night the bugler stood by the flagpole, and his notes in taps rang out cleanly in the crisp, cold air. They echoed faintly and mournfully to the Sick Bay room of Horst Hedmann. The lights were out, and it was in shadows. Hedmann was propped up on his pillow, listening to the bugler, but thinking of another land and another people, and a war of which he was no longer a part.

The clear, sad notes were closer to Shuford, and he looked up from the papers on his desk.

His room was smaller, but furnished like those in which Hedmann, Bauer, and Schlisser would be lodged in the morning. It was down the passageway from Hedmann's room. The desk was littered with pictures and diagrams and dominated by a large, illustrated side view of a U-85 type, marked, of course, TOP SECRET. It had been smuggled out of Germany in 1940.

Also on the desk edge was an electric teapot, a poor substitute for that hallowed brown vessel that had vanished in a London air raid. There was also a stained cup, and a full ashtray was in evidence, stubs of Players cigarettes sticking up like stumps on a shelled battlefield.

Shuford felt inadequate to the complex technical job, and his eyes were red and weary. He had not left the room since the forenoon. He listened to the final phrasing drawn from the bugler's lips until there were goose bumps on his arms, then he bent over the illustrated side view again.

When taps penetrated their bunkroom, the yeomen had fallen silent for reasons they did not know. They'd been confined to the intelligence compound, under orders not to leave it until released by Lieutenant Shuford. As the last notes faded out, Kesler said, "The lieutenant thinks we'll go to work tomorrow. Four on and four off, around the clock."

"I'll be ready," Honig said.

"We're as much prisoners here as those damn Nazis," Schroder said.

"You think we'll ever see them?" Goldberg asked no one in particular.

"The only thing we're going to do is sit and listen, four hours on, four hours off," Kesler said. "The lieutenant said he wants anything the prisoners say to be recorded, written down in stenotype and handwritten. He said if they even sneeze, write it down."

"How about a belch?" Schroder asked.

That got a laugh.

"That, too," said Kesler. "Shuford said not to miss a single word."

"Even if they whisper?" Goldberg asked.

"Even if they whisper," Kesler replied.

The bunkroom soon became silent.

The day dawned clear across the approaches to Hampton Roads. The sky was cloudless, and the sun was attacking the snowy beard of frost on the grass blades inside the quadrangle as the German survivors were herded through the steel-wire fence and into the barracks. They'd already had breakfast in Sick Bay.

Soon Horst Hedmann, in new clothing—khaki shirt and pants—was examining his room. He laughed softly as he disconnected a microphone in the wall switch, using his blunt fingernail to turn the screw and replace the plate. He'd already found the mikes in the ceiling fixture and in the heating unit, but not the one in the steam line. He looked carefully around the room and then went to the wall, calling in a barely audible whisper, "Bauer! Bauer!"

After a few seconds, he heard Bauer's whispered, "Yes, *Kapitän*."

Hedmann moved to the door between the rooms and tried the knob. To his amazement, the door wasn't locked. He opened it, a suspicious smile on his face. Bauer stepped in.

"I don't understand," Hedmann said, his eyes sharpening in distrust. "They don't lock the door? They put us in adjoining rooms?" He went to the window and stared out across the sunlit quadrangle. Despite the high steel fence, it all seemed too much a slice of freedom. Then he turned again to Bauer. "But I do understand, Bauer." He nodded confidently.

"What, sir?"

Hedmann finally smiled. "They are trying to confuse us and soften us. Did you check your room for microphones? I found three in here and disconnected them."

Bauer said, "I found one."

Fifteen doors away, in the opposite wing, was the monitoring room. There were several loudspeakers in it tuned to conversational level, and three desks. Kesler was at one and Honig manned another. Shuford sat on the edge of Kesler's desk, looking at a speaker and listening. Recordings were being made, but Shuford wouldn't risk a breakdown. Over the speakers, Hedmann's voice could be heard: "Whenever we talk, we'll use this room. But neither of us will discuss anything to do with the war, or the homeland, and particularly not the submarines. Do you understand, Bauer?"

Bauer's voice replied, "I do."

Hedmann closed the door to Bauer's room and motioned his second officer to be seated. He remained standing. With a sigh, he said, "I think the navy captain and the Britisher have decided that Schlisser is the weakest. They separated us, probably, to give him a feeling of insecurity." Hedmann turned to the window. "It would have been better if he had died."

Bauer looked down at the floor. "So many died."

Hedmann nodded. "One more would not have made a difference, then."

There was a firm knock at the door, and Shuford

entered with the air of a doctor making his morning rounds. Bauer immediately leaped to attention.

"Good morning. Are you comfortable?" Shuford asked cordially.

Hedmann smiled. "Too comfortable, Lieutenant . . . ?"

"Shuford."

"Too disturbingly comfortable, Lieutenant Shuford," he said.

"The Allies do not mistreat prisoners of war, especially combat men."

Hedmann scanned the room. "But this hardly feels like a prison."

Shuford moved slowly toward the wide window and peered out. "You've noticed the high fence and patrols. You're well confined, and in time you'll be removed to a regular prisoner-of-war camp here in Virginia. After a certain amount of interrogation, of course."

Hedmann smiled at the word "interrogation" and then glanced at Bauer. He said, in German, "Would you excuse us, please, Bauer?"

The second officer nodded with military sharpness, and then he swiftly retreated from the room.

When the door clicked shut, Hedmann said admiringly, "An excellent officer, Bauer. He almost saved us after my mistake of going into water too shallow. I was greedy, Lieutenant Shuford. I had dreams of another big, fat tanker."

Then he lapsed into silence and Shuford waited him out, that one good eye fastened on the clean jawline of the sub captain.

Hedmann began again briskly, "Now, about interrogation—I must say it once again. Under Geneva, you can only force my men and myself to give you a name, rank, and serial number.''

"I wish Germany would also observe Geneva and other humane conduct in, say, such things as attacking neutral ships, gunning men in lifeboats, and fire-bombing civilian populations," Shuford commented. "I've heard some disturbing things about your treatment of German Jews."

"My orders were to sink Allied shipping. That I have done," Hedmann responded coldly.

"Quite well, I may say."

Hedmann walked to the bedside radio and turned it on. "I think you will find that sinking ships is not quite as dirty a business as intelligence."

Shuford nodded. "I might also be inclined to agree with you."

Concert music faded in on the radio, and Hedmann adjusted the dial for tone. He listened briefly and then said, "I spent a few months in England once. In the summer. It is very beautiful in your country. Somewhat like the land near Hamburg. My home is in Wandsbeck."

"I know it well," Shuford said.

The music was now "Greensleeves," with the sound of a hundred violins sweeping through the old English air.

Hedmann glanced at the radio again. "Lovely music, that. Typically English. Flowers and green grass. I haven't really thought about them for a long time."

"It's one of my favorites, too," Shuford said, struggling to grasp the inside of this man.

"It tells us what life could be like, doesn't it?" said Hedmann. Then he held out his hands and looked at them. "Would you believe it—I played in a string group until two years ago. Cello. Not professional, of course. For enjoyment only."

"Cello? Did you, now? I played in a stodgy string quartet at Oxford. Violin."

"You read music?"

Shuford nodded.

"Well"—Hedmann grinned—"we have something to discuss besides this present plight."

The U-boat commander sat down on the edge of his bed and Shuford offered him a cigarette. He accepted gladly.

"Do you have any?" Shuford asked.

"No."

Shuford stepped to the door and spoke to the guard. "Get a carton of cigarettes for each of our guests, and please relay to Captain Haines my request for three bottles of the best brandy you have in the officers' mess."

The guard blinked, mumbled, "Yes, sir," and moved off.

"That is very kind of you," said Hedmann.

Shuford settled into a chair. "Our pleasure. Now, *Kapitän* Hedmann, about sixty days ago off the Delaware breakwater, one of the American destroyers got a definite sonar contact on a German submarine. But before he could even run up on the sub, he got such confusion in his sound system that he—"

Hedmann looked away. "My name is Horst Hedmann. I am a *Kapitänleutnant* in the German navy. My serial number is five-one-six-two-zero."

Shuford went on, "He lost contact—"

"My name is Horst Hedmann. I am a *Kapitänleutnant* in the German navy. My serial number is five-one-six-two-zero."

Shuford was relentless. "We also know that this sub came south and used the same tactics—"

"My name is Horst Hedmann—"

Shuford sucked in a deep, annoyed breath. Further interrogation at this time would be futile, he knew. "I'll drop that line of questioning."

Hedmann smiled warmly. "That is better, Lieutenant. We should talk about music, or literature, or gardening. Ah, gardening. I love roses."

Shuford was amused. "That is safe for you."

"And so much more enjoyable."

Shuford studied the German. "You certainly don't have any of the outward trappings of a Nazi. You haven't *heil*ed Hitler once or popped your heels."

"That would be ridiculous, wouldn't it? I am an alien, in an alien land. If you were a prisoner of war in Germany, would you constantly go around shouting, 'God save the king'?"

Shuford laughed. "Not unless I wanted to attract attention."

"Exactly."

Shuford was silent a moment and then said thoughtfully, "You've proved something to me this morning."

Hedmann was curious. "What have I proved?"

"That submarine men aren't necessarily of a type."

"Oh, you'll find all types."

"I suppose. But you, at least, seem to have many dimensions."

Hedmann smiled. "Oddly enough, I never thought about submarines until eight years ago. I wanted to be a fisherman, own my own trawler in the North Sea, and live on a bluff above the Elbe." There was a thoughtful pause. "Such foolish notions."

Shuford arose. "Not foolish, but pretty much knocked about at this stage. Are you married?"

"Yes, I have a wife and two children. They live at Blankenese. Over the Elbe. They were there the last I heard. Are you married?"

Shuford's face suddenly became grave. "Not now."

Hedmann answered with a sigh. "There will be better days."

"If we have *our* way, yes," Shuford agreed with him, smiling again.

Hedmann stood up and bowed slightly. "You have me at a great disadvantage in answering you."

"I spent a Christmas in Germany once, long ago. My wife and son were with me. My daughter hadn't been born. A wonderful Christmas, *Kapitän* Hedmann. We spent it with a family in Bremerhaven."

"Close to us."

Shuford nodded. "I remember the smells in that kitchen. *Lebkuchen* and *Stollen*. Superb."

"Umm," said the submariner, relieved that the subject had been changed.

"We all went to church Christmas Eve, and as soon as we returned, the mother of that family opened the door to the parlor, where the tree was set up. The children had not seen the tree, with all its white candles burning, until that very moment. Then she played the piano while we all sang '*O Tannenbaum.*' "

" 'O Christmas Tree.' " Hedmann sighed and nodded. "A typical German Christmas."

It occurred to Shuford that if Horst Hedmann did have a soft spot, family was it. *Natural*, he thought, *that's how it should be*.

Hedmann sighed. "And here I am, far from home."

"I'm afraid you are. So am I. We'll make the best of it, eh?"

Hedmann nodded again, but it was evident to Shuford that his thoughts were in Hamburg, perhaps on the large advent wreaths that hung this week in the windows of German homes. At least, before the war they'd hung there. Perhaps Hedmann's home had been bombed, too. A sobering thought.

Shuford turned to leave. "I will question Schlisser now."

Hedmann frowned. "Why not Bauer?"

Shuford smiled, standing on the threshold. "I'm a very democratic man. First an officer, then an enlisted man."

When Shuford's footsteps had echoed down the passageway, Hedmann clenched his fists until the tendons across the knuckles turned white.

In the monitoring room the speakers became silent. Kesler looked at them for a moment and then turned to Honig.

"Strange they'd be talking about Christmas, kitchen smells, and the tree. We're at war, they're enemies . . ."

"Enemies know it's coming."

"Yeah, but right now I'm thinking about Hedmann saying it would be better if Schlisser wasn't here, not about Christmas."

Honig nodded, recalling the conversation.

"Didn't that sound like Hedmann thinks Schlisser might crack?"

"Shuford said Schlisser is younger than we are."

"And if Shuford puts enough pressure on him?"

Honig said, "He might crack."

"I hope so," Kesler said. "Isn't that why we're here?"

"Yeah."

Shuford was with Schlisser from eleven to four o'clock, with a break for lunch. At four o'clock, bathed in sweat, Schlisser pleaded once again, "I know nothing. I am back with the torpedoes. I know nothing." He'd been saying that for four hours. His eighteen-year-old face was tortured.

Shuford had asked the same question fifty different ways. But Schlisser was the son of a farmer in the Holstein province and his mind was an absolute miracle of simplicity. "I stay by my battle station, I do nothing," Schlisser answered for the fifty-first time.

Shuford sighed. "All right, Schlisser. I brought you something. I know this has been a difficult twenty-four hours for you." He dug into the bag beside him and extracted a bottle of brandy. "This may help you sleep tonight. We are not inhuman, you know."

Schlisser looked at the brown bottle suspiciously. "It is doped," he said.

Shuford did not answer him but uncapped the bottle, took a long swig, and put the bottle on the table. "We will both be doped."

"I know nothing," Schlisser said feverishly. "I am a torpedoman, third."

Shuford nodded and stepped out toward the passageway and walked tiredly toward the monitoring room. Captain Haines was there, with Geiger and Goldberg.

"Any sign of a break?" Haines asked.

"You must have heard it all, Captain," Shuford answered.

"I did. You talked about music and flowers and Christmas with Hedmann. You spent five hours with that boy and got nothing. You gave away three bottles of brandy—"

"I learned that Schlisser is the one who won't crack," Shuford said defensively.

"And *how* did you learn that?" Haines asked.

"His rules are simple and unchangeable. I'll concentrate on Bauer and Hedmann."

"Well, you better damn sight start concentrating, then," Haines snapped.

"As the war goes on, Captain Haines, I think you will find that patience is the best asset in this work."

"There's no time for patience," Captain Haines roared. "The Atlantic Fleet Command reported three more subs in the Eastern Sea Frontier. They're sinking three ships a day—sometimes four. They're all equipped with this devilish device. And to give this a personal turn, it won't be long before they equip the subs off England."

"I need time, Captain," Shuford said. "More than your forty-eight hours."

Haines walked out without replying.

The loudspeaker crackled, and Shuford swiveled his head toward it.

Bauer's voice came out: "I wonder why he didn't get to me today?"

Geiger was writing furiously in shorthand.

Hedmann's voice: "Maybe he's saving you for tonight. He questioned Schlisser after me. I'm worried."

Bauer's voice: "But, sir, Schlisser knows absolutely nothing."

Hedmann's voice: "True, and not true."

Goldberg's fingers were flying on the stenotype machine.

Bauer's voice: "I don't understand."

Hedmann's voice: "Let me set up a hypothetical circumstance. The lieutenant goes to Schlisser with essentially harmless information. He says, 'Hedmann told me such and such, and so and so . . . !' "

Shuford's eyes narrowed.

The voice continued: "And so poor Schlisser thinks to himself, 'Well, if the *Kapitän* told him that, I cannot dispute it.' So poor Schlisser affirms what the Britisher has put into my mouth . . . and further, Bauer, speaking of a piece of equipment, he tells them how it works. Schlisser knows more than he appears to know."

Bauer's voice: "I understand now."

Hedmann's voice: "A very simple trap for Schlisser."

Then there was a pause.

Hedmann: "It is a shame that the bright lieutenant with the dead eye—the noncombatant—doesn't prefer to match wits with me all the way." There was a pause.

Clay Shuford knew that Horst Hedmann was speaking directly to him.

Shuford said tiredly to the voice, "I knew it the moment I saw you on the deck of that tug."

The speaker crackled again. "And, Lieutenant Shuford, because I have the feeling that you are listening somewhere, what I have just described is an interrogation technique as old as Hannibal. You use it. We use it. But it doesn't always work."

Shuford could picture him standing in the center

of the room like an actor delivering a precurtain speech, his face a mask of defiance.

"Match wits with me, not Schlisser!" Hedmann shouted. "I will enjoy it, Professor."

Then the speaker became silent, and Shuford blew out a long breath.

Kesler removed his hovering hands from the stenotype; he was watching Shuford. "That's a rough customer."

"Very rough."

"What do we do now?"

"I'm afraid that's what Captain Haines is asking, too. I'm not quite sure what to do, First."

"You could always call in a couple of healthy marines."

"That would indeed make Captain Haines happy," Shuford said.

Captain Haines was readying to go home, and his secretary extracted the papers from his out-basket. They were all marked TOP SECRET.

She asked, "You've read this, sir?" She held the transcript of Hedmann's interrogation in the morning.

"Yes, send it to Washington on tonight's courier plane," Haines muttered. "What there is of it."

The phone rang and Haines picked it up. "Cap'n Haines here."

A yeoman was on the other end, then an admiral's aide, then Rear Admiral Goddard. "What's happening down there?" Goddard was in Washington, Chief of ONI.

"Very little, sir," Haines replied.

"Well, speed it up. We're taking a bad beating."

Haines nodded into the phone. "Yes, sir. But

frankly, Admiral, I'm disappointed in the man you sent down for this." Haines rotated his chair so that his back was to the open door and he was looking into the red twilight through his window.

Just then Shuford appeared at Haines's door but stopped suddenly, realizing that he was being discussed. He moved back into the outer office but could still hear Haines: "He's not the type to get anywhere with this. He's a British college instructor and doesn't know a submarine from a log canoe."

Shuford stood frozen outside the door, his one good eye closed as the words cut into him cruelly.

"There must be an interrogation expert up there who knows something about submarines," Haines continued. "On top of that, this fellow believes in handling these Heinies with kid gloves. I don't."

Then the admiral replied, and of course Shuford couldn't hear what he was saying; but Shuford guessed that he agreed rather completely with the submarine captain.

"I'll keep you advised, Admiral, but please ask them to send me a combat man for this job. *Now!* This is a technical thing we're seeking."

There was another brief exchange and then Haines hung up, snorting, "Oxford, for God's sake!"

Shuford was still standing outside the captain's door when the secretary came through it and stopped, reddening. "Lieutenant, I don't think he meant anything personal."

"I'm sure he didn't," Shuford answered. "He just wanted to bolster my confidence." He had changed his mind about seeing the captain, and left.

He'd decided to use a yeoman for direct contact with the enlisted German. He'd wanted Haines's approval but now decided to go ahead without it.

*   *   *

Kesler pushed Schlisser's door open at five-thirty, bringing in the evening meal. Schlisser, still nervous and exhausted from the interrogation, motioned to the yeoman to place the tray on the table. Shuford had told Kesler to make friends with him; Kesler did not look like an enemy. He looked Pennsylvania Dutch, a cow milker.

Kesler said cheerfully, speaking in German, "Stew! And it not only stinks like old socks but it was made from old socks. I may even go to that prison camp with you to get away from this cook." He took the tin cover off the plate. "Look at that mess. *Phewwwww!*"

Schlisser grinned timidly and approached the table.

Kesler said, "I hear this cook is first-class, striking for chief. Gonna make a big name for himself. Economy! Chief Make-a-Meal-for-Nothing! Cooks rocks that look like dumplings but taste like rocks."

Schlisser said amiably, "It does not look so bad to me."

Kesler sat down on Schlisser's bed to observe the prisoner. He said, "Go ahead, eat. Be paralyzed."

Schlisser took a spoonful. "It's good."

"*Eeeeeaaaaah!* If that's good, you must have had a real lousy cook on that U-boat. Lucky he's not going to be around to pass out indigestion."

Schlisser took the spoon from his mouth and looked over at Kesler, hurt and grieving. He had a kind face with round, full, rosy cheeks, like those seen in München beer ads. "I'm sorry that anyone went down with it," he said.

Kesler wished he could pull the words out of the air again. "And I'm sorry I said that. I was just trying to cheer you up. Food's always a good gag, your navy or mine."

Schlisser smiled and resumed slurping up the stew.

"Anything you need in here?" Kesler asked.

"No, but it is a little lonely. I wonder why they are keeping me away from my *Kapitän*."

Kesler shrugged. "You know, rank and all that. You're a peon, like me."

Schlisser said worriedly, "I thought maybe it was because they thought I would talk if I were not near the commander."

"I really don't know," Kesler replied truthfully.

Schlisser put his spoon down. "I will *not* talk. I will not tell the lieutenant anything about the boat. I will not tell *you* anything. I can keep secrets."

Kesler laughed. "You're over my head now, German sailor. That's for the brass and braid." But the laugh covered a different thought: *You may be close to being right about your* Kapitän.

Schlisser continued, "I was thinking last night that *Kapitän* Hedmann would feel safer if I weren't here. If I were down in that boat with the rest, I could never talk—"

"Don't say that nonsense," Kesler advised.

Schlisser thought a moment and then nodded. "Yes, you're right. It was lonely here last night. I think when I'm alone."

Kesler pulled up off the bed. "I better go now. Confidentially, there's a hamburger joint just outside the gate. Dime each. I'm gonna eat . . . eat . . . eat . . . before I go on watch." That was a lie, of course.

Schlisser grinned at last. "Thank you for the food, and for talking to me."

Kesler smiled back. "Don't mention it. We'll talk again."

He went down the passageway and knocked on Shuford's door. Caught in the middle of letter writing, the lieutenant welcomed the yeoman in.

"I talked to Schlisser for a few minutes," Kesler said.

"Say anything worthwhile?"

"Said he wouldn't tell you anything about the boat; nor me."

"And I'm sure he won't," said Shuford.

"Do you think *Kapitän* Hedmann would kill Schlisser if he had a chance?" Kesler asked. "Just to keep him from talking?"

"Why do you ask?"

"He seemed scared. He's lonely. He wonders why you aren't letting him see his commander. I don't think he understands all of this kind treatment to a prisoner of war."

Shuford sat back in his chair thoughtfully. "Anything else?"

"He said he thought the *Kapitän* would feel safer if he weren't here, if he'd gone down with the boat."

Shuford nodded. "He may be right."

Then, noticing a framed picture on Shuford's desk—an attractive woman and two smiling children—Kesler asked, "Your family?"

Shuford glanced at the picture. "They *were* my family. My wife and twelve-year-old daughter were killed in the third big raid on London. Germans dropped incendiaries. I think they died quickly and without too much pain. The fire was so hot that it sucked the oxygen right out of the air. I was not at home that night. I had duty at Whitehall. I often wish

I had been at home." Shuford looked away from the photo.

Then he looked back.

"War doesn't choose its victims very well. My son, about your age, was lost on the HMS *Cybillis*. Convoy duty off Scotland. Only five survivors. A German submarine . . ." His voice trailed away.

Kesler said, "I'm sorry," for the second time within ten minutes.

Shuford nodded and after Kesler had gone, he wrote on his notepad, "Schlisser thinks Hedmann might want to kill him."

Then he looked for a long time at the photograph on his desk and thought about his deceased family. Tears came. He wondered why he did not feel a blind rage toward the three German POWs.

The yeomen, off duty, ate at a separate table in the ONI mess, away from other enlisted personnel. Their food was brought over from the base general mess.

Kesler sat with Geiger. He said, "When the lieutenant told me to take Schlisser his food I thought I'd want to dump it over his head. But the minute I saw him up close he was just like me. So I made a joke of it. Then a crazy thing happened—I felt sorry for him. He's just like everybody else. He got caught up in this war like we did."

"Yeah, but you know he fires torpedoes," Geiger said. "We just push pencils."

"Look, I'll bet he didn't ask for submarines. He just got them."

Geiger shrugged.

"The only reason you're sitting here and I'm sitting here is that we speak German. Otherwise we might both be on destroyers or even submarines. So what he does is not his fault. It's the fault of the war.''

"You gonna get buddy-buddy with him?" Geiger asked.

"I wouldn't mind," Kesler said. "He's scared to death."

By 9:00 P.M., both Haines and Shuford were showing wear. They'd been listening in the monitor room since just after dinner.

The watch had changed. Honig and Schroder were now on duty. Though Kesler was off duty, he couldn't stay away from the monitoring room.

Haines rose and stretched. "There hasn't been a sound on those speakers in two hours," he said. "I'm going home."

"Good idea, sir. One thing more. I've been thinking that Hedmann would make contact with Schlisser if he could. It might be interesting to hear their conversation."

Haines frowned. "It was your decision to place Schlisser in a room away from the other two."

"I'm going to conveniently pull the guards away from all the rooms after midnight. The prisoners can't escape from this compound. These inside guards are window dressing."

Kesler stared at Shuford in disbelief. Hadn't the lieutenant heard him say that Schlisser was afraid that Hedmann would kill him? Hadn't the lieutenant read the transcript and seen that the commander had said it would have been better if Schlisser was dead?

Haines stopped in the middle of putting on his heavy coat with the striped shoulder boards and gleaming old buttons. "I think you're taking a debatable risk," he said.

"As you wish, sir," Shuford said quietly.

"How is Hedmann supposed to know which room Schlisser is in?"

"The empty guard chair by the door."

Haines pulled the greatcoat over his massive shoulders and shook his head. "I don't know about this," he said miserably.

"When the guard is relieved outside Hedmann's door at midnight," Shuford continued, "I'll have him say that you think the passageway guards are unnecessary and you are securing them for the night."

A look of helpless consternation dropped over the captain's choppy face. "I'm saying that?" He stared at the British intelligence officer with disgust. The look as much as said that he believed that the intelligence lieutenant was a blithering idiot.

The captain shook his head. It was all too much for him. All he wanted to do was fight a war, shoot some holes in the sides of Japanese ships. "All right, Shuford," he said, "but all three of those men better be in their rooms when I come back in the morning. I'm looking silly enough now without having to report their escape. Bottles of brandy? Cigarettes? My god." He stomped off.

"Good-night, sir," said Shuford.

Kesler departed for his bunk. He had the midnight watch.

At 2:00 A.M., the loudspeakers were still silent. Shuford was dozing on his cot in the monitor room. Kesler and Goldberg were playing acey-deucey.

But down the passageway, *Kapitänleutnant* Horst Hedmann was wide awake. He'd been alternately staring out of the window and pacing since midnight, when the strange conversation had taken place outside his door. He could not comprehend the reason why Captain Haines had removed the passage guards. Yet it was all of the same easy, lunatic pattern. No locked doors; brandy, cigarettes. Almost a country club. Finally, he attributed it to the remarkable nonchalance of the Americans—and for that matter, the British, too. They were maddening, baffling races of people.

He walked across the room and listened with his ear against the door. Then he opened it gently and scanned the empty passageway. He looked at the empty chair by his door, then at the one at Bauer's door, and finally, the lonely one way down the passage by Schlisser's door. He drew his head back inside, his face creased in perplexity, and stood for a moment in the partial shadows by his door. Then he opened it and moved down the passage, padding barefoot.

Schlisser was asleep and appeared to be in a stupor. Hedmann spotted the half-empty brandy bottle on the floor and picked it up, sloshing it around. Then he looked down at the torpedoman. The round face and rosy cheeks were innocent in slumber; the mouth was slack and emitted a watery snore. *Schlisser is weak*, Hedmann thought, *and the professor will soon reduce him to babble. He'll talk about the* Unterseeboot.

Hedmann replaced the bottle by the bed, took a deep, steadying breath, and his lips moved in prayer: "God save his soul. God grant him peace."

Then Horst Hedmann bent over slightly and raised his powerful right arm. With a vicious and practiced downward blow, the palm of his right hand crashed into Schlisser's neck.

There was a grunt. It was a stunning if not fatal blow. The sailor's drunkenness had relaxed him.

Quickly, the *Kapitänleutnant* placed a chair under the overhead steam line and then tied the notched end of Schlisser's belt to it after making a loop with the buckle. He carried the torpedoman's body to the chair and pulled it erect with brute strength, until the loop of the belt was under Schlisser's chin. Then he stood back and kicked the chair from beneath the body. The farm boy from Holstein died within seconds.

In the monitoring room, Kesler paused, his head toward the speakers, his hand holding a peg poised over the acey-deucey board. "I thought I heard something," he said.

"Come on now, Otto," Goldberg replied testily. "Don't stall."

Frowning widely, Kesler held up his hand for silence, then said, "Wake the lieutenant . . ."

Hedmann shook Bauer, who came to in confusion.

Suddenly alert, Bauer whispered, "Yes, *Kapitän*."

Hedmann sat down on the edge of Bauer's bed. He said quietly, "I could not sleep. I wanted to talk to you."

"Yes, *Kapitän*."

Hedmann said, "Remember, Bauer, when I took command of the boat at Kiel? I talked to the men and said that some of us might have to give full sacrifice."

"Yes, *Kapitän*." Bauer was concerned. He had never seen the commander like this.

Hedmann took a deep breath. "There are not

many of us left now." Then he faltered and rubbed his eyes. "But you and I must not crack."

Shuford was now wide awake and back in the monitoring room, listening to the barely audible voices on the loudspeaker. "What's this all about?" Goldberg asked.

"Quiet," Shuford whispered.

They heard Hedmann say, "I did not make many wrong decisions on the boat, Bauer, did I? Most of them were right."

Bauer's anxious voice came out: "Are you trying to tell me something, *Kapitän*? Some bad news?"

Hedmann stood up from the bed and Bauer started to slip out of it. Hedmann waved him back. "Stay where you are, Bauer. I'm going back to my room in a moment."

He began to pace the room, and then he stopped to face his second officer. "I'm trying to tell you, Bauer, that a boat commander's duty does not stop when his boat is shot out from under him. He must still protect it from the enemy."

"But, *Kapitän*, the boat is in forty fathoms of water. It is protected by the sea."

"But *we* are vulnerable, you and I," said Hedmann, his voice rising. *"We are!"*

"I will not talk, believe me, *Kapitän*," Bauer promised earnestly.

Hedmann stared at him through the dim light. "I don't think you will, Bauer. But whatever happens in the next two or three days, remember that a boat commander's duty does not cease when his boat is lost."

"Yes, *Kapitän*," Bauer said.

"Good-night."

Then the loudspeaker went mute, leaving Shuford gaping at it.

Goldberg broke the spell. "That squarehead sounds goofy to me."

"Not to me," Shuford said thoughtfully.

"The way he talks, you'd think he left the family heirlooms on that boat," Goldberg continued.

"Never mind the way he talks," Shuford said. "He's a real man, a fighting man. Something that we apparently *are not*. Now transcribe that conversation for me to study in the morning . . ."

The lieutenant paused outside the door of the monitoring room and looked toward Schlisser's doorway. He could not bring himself to walk down and open it. He went on to bed but did not sleep.

Kesler discovered Schlisser's body when he brought the breakfast tray at 7:00 A.M., and within ten minutes it was beneath a blanket on the floor. The empty belt loop still dangled from the hot steam line.

The doctor who had been summoned said to Shuford, "We'll do an autopsy in a few hours, but from what I can see, he was well on his way to dying before any strangulation took place. I think he was also quite drunk. How does a drunk climb up and hang himself?"

Shuford tried to appear surprised. "It isn't suicide, you say. How then?"

"Just a hunch, Lieutenant, but I'd say a very expert judo hand broke his neck with a single blow," the doctor said, looking down at the motionless form beneath the blanket. "Not a suicide here."

"That's hard to believe," said Shuford, calmly. "Please call me when the autopsy is finished."

"I know you have a strange operation here and it's none of my business, Lieutenant, but aren't these prisoners guarded at night?"

Shuford eyed the doctor. "It is none of your business."

A moment later, Shuford was on the mat in Captain Haines's office.

"This is the final result of your insane interrogation methods. Murder! I'm sorry I listened to you. It was murder, not suicide, I tell you."

Shuford nodded blithely. "You're quite right, sir. It was murder. I regret it very much. Of course, I accept full responsibility for what happened to Schlisser." Shuford sounded more British than ever. Stiff upper lip.

Haines was openmouthed, almost in a state of shock. "You accept full responsibility?" he said, with a laugh descended from a coyote's. "I'll pass that along to the admiral, by God. The first three submarine prisoners in American waters, and I let one of them be murdered." His voice rose to a shout. "I'll pass it along, and it's a pretty damned weird report I've got to make."

Shuford maintained his calm. "Captain, I seriously hope you won't forget the objective of this whole affair. To get information that will save other lives, other ships. *Allied lives, Allied ships—not German lives*."

His attitude and subdued manner rocked Haines back. "Schlisser might have talked."

"No, sir," Shuford said emphatically. "Schlisser would never have talked. I'm sure of that."

Haines thought for a moment, and then his eyes drilled into the British officer and his voice became low and demanding. "Did you have any idea that Hedmann might go this far?"

"The possibility occurred to me," Shuford readily admitted.

Haines gasped. "You didn't mention it last night."

"Sir, I'll mention the possibility now that Schlisser's death might be the key to what we want. Hedmann, underneath, is a very gentle man with a deep conscience of what is right and wrong. He did his duty, and it will weigh heavily upon him now, and we'll take advantage. Today."

Haines's eyes narrowed suddenly. "Mr. Shuford, did you plot that death?"

"'Plot' is hardly the right word, Captain Haines," the lieutenant replied.

Haines sank down into his chair. In a voice that was almost ill, he asked, "What kind of man are you?"

Shuford's one good eye was steady on the American captain. "I'm a civilian college instructor caught up in a total war," he said.

Haines slumped back in his chair. "And I thought I was cold blooded."

"Until three years ago I thought I was warm blooded. Then I held the bodies of my wife and daughter in my arms. Two years ago I attended a memorial service for my son in Portsmouth, victim of a submarine attack."

Captain Haines looked down at his desk and began shuffling papers, his anger returning. "I'm putting Hedmann in the brig and I'll ask the judge-advocate how to handle the charges, what to do. Then I want you relieved."

"Nothing can bring the enlisted man back," Shuford said quietly. "Play along with Hedmann. Accept the death as suicide. Otherwise you'll lose the game, Captain."

Captain Haines was still in shock.

"You do want something to report to Washington, don't you, sir?" Shuford continued with icy calm.

Captain Haines laughed bitterly and adjusted the dolphin emblem on the front of his desk. It had been crooked and Haines was a very shipshape man. Finally he nodded.

"Thank you very much, Captain."

As the lieutenant was leaving to see Hedmann, Haines looked after him and said, "I suddenly realized that my baseball bat is just a feather. But I'm now proud of that, Mr. Shuford. I don't plot death."

Shuford departed silently.

Kesler was in the enlisted mess hall. "I almost knew it was going to happen." His face was drawn and tired.

"Didn't you tell Shuford?" Schroder asked.

"I told him. I told him that Schlisser thought Hedmann would kill him. I told him that the day before yesterday."

"What did he say?"

"Not much. I know he read the transcripts."

Schroder frowned. "That guy must have ice water in his veins."

"I guess he does," Kesler replied. "Schlisser seemed to be OK, even if he was enemy."

"Why didn't Shuford move him out of here? I heard he even removed the guards."

"I can't answer that." But that was a lie. Kesler did know. Schlisser was murdered by both Hedmann and Shuford.

"Good morning, *Kapitän*," Shuford said pleasantly, entering Hedmann's room.

Hedmann was equally cheerful. "Good morning to you, Lieutenant Shuford," he replied.

"Did you sleep well?" Shuford asked.

Hedmann shook his head. "I had a period of wakefulness. I talked to Bauer, as I'm sure your monitors reported. I give you all credit for the concealment of microphones. I've checked this room a hundred times, and Bauer's, too. Yet I know I'm tapped."

"It's a shame about Schlisser's death," Shuford replied.

Hedmann's expression changed and his eyes grew remote. "Yes, the yeoman told me when he delivered breakfast. I think, perhaps, that the pressure here was too much for him. Poor boy. Suicide."

"Poor boy," Shuford agreed, and then remained silent.

"In a way," Hedmann continued, "you are to blame. You must have been unethical in your questioning yesterday."

Shuford opened the cover of the notebook he was carrying and folded it back. "I might have been," he admitted. "I'm sorry for his death."

"Of course, I must report this to the International Red Cross," Hedmann pointed out. "And I shall want, naturally, to discuss burial arrangements and such with your chaplain. Schlisser's death should be reported to my command in France, as well, by the Red Cross."

"That is your privilege, *Kapitän* Hedmann."

Then Hedmann brightened. "You have a note-book in your hand. What do we have today? Is it my turn?"

"I will question Heinrich Bauer."

Hedmann grinned. "I wish you luck."

Then as Shuford placed his hand on the doorknob to Bauer's room, Hedmann began to softly whistle "*O Tannenbaum, O Tannenbaum.*"

Shuford paused, staring at Hedmann, but then proceeded into Bauer's room, closing the door firmly behind him.

Kesler could not stay out of the monitoring room. He was becoming obsessed with the battle between Hedmann and Lieutenant Shuford. He could think of little else. It was a game of minds, the British lieutenant using his as a knife and the German commander using his as a shield.

Honig said, "I called my girlfriend last night and had to bite my tongue when she asked what I was doing." They were under orders not to discuss what was happening in the ONI compound.

Kesler said, "How long can it last?"

"Until one of them cracks, of course," said Gold-berg.

Voices began again on the speakers.

From the start, Bauer showed signs of extreme nervousness. Shuford had seen them all. Bauer pulled at his shirt tabs, blew his sharp nose, lit a cigarette with a shaking hand. Bauer was the one with outward Nazi leanings. He was the only one who'd *Heil, Hitler*ed. Shuford made a guess that he'd come up from the line from the dictator's *Lederhosen*ed *Jugend* groups, the youth groups.

"Relax, *Herr* Bauer," Shuford advised. "We may have many of these sessions."

"You are wasting your time," Bauer said. "Why don't you send us off to prison camp?"

Shuford smiled warmly. "That will follow." Then he arranged the notebook on his knee and began, "Now, from the information I have, via British intelligence, you sailed from Lorient early in November, operated around the Azores for a week, then returned to France to resupply, and set off for the American coast on November twenty-sixth."

"Your information is wrong."

"You sank a ship off the Massachusetts coast and then proceeded south and got a tanker, the *Charles Smith*, off the New Jersey coast."

Bauer raked his muscular hands through his dark, curly hair. "I won't answer your questions."

"These aren't questions, *Herr* Bauer. I'm simply telling you what I already know."

"You know nothing," Bauer said. "You only guess."

Shuford went on calmly. "On or about December sixteenth, you made the Cape Hatteras area."

Bauer was now angry, something Hedmann would not have permitted in himself. "I do not have to listen to you," he said curtly. "And I will not, do you hear?"

Shuford smiled. "You have little choice, my friend. You are a prisoner of war."

In the monitoring room, their voices carried over the loudspeaker, the conversation entirely in German. The stenotype was busy; Honig was scribbling.

Goldberg glanced up from the stenotype. "That lieutenant sure knows how to keep cool."

"Then on December nineteenth, you attacked the *Malay Queen* and the *Ethel Sinclair*, and late that afternoon were attacked by the USS *Blevins* . . ."

"My name is Heinrich Bauer . . ."

The wall clock over Kesler's shoulder clicked to 9:30 A.M. as Shuford continued. "We believe your eventual operating area, prior to sailing back to France, was Hampton Roads traffic, out off Cape Henry . . ."

In his room, *Kapitänleutnant* Horst Hedmann paced restlessly, looking occasionally at Bauer's door. He was tempted to stand by it and listen but would not chance the embarrassment of being caught there, should the lieutenant open it suddenly.

By ten-thirty, Bauer had lost some of his nervous petulance and had begun to stiffen noticeably.

"Now, I understand you were able to operate three to four weeks if you conserved fuel," Shuford said.

"You will learn nothing from me," Bauer said.

"Well, we'll spend the day talking pleasantly about nothing, then," Shuford replied amiably.

When the hands of the clock in the monitor room were straight up, Bauer asked impatiently, "Do you plan to starve me, too?"

Shuford looked at his watch. "How inconsiderate of me," he said, and gently folded his notebook.

As Shuford passed through Hedmann's room, the German officer queried, with a pretense of total unconcern, "Would it be possible to have a daily paper? I do like to keep up with the news."

"Yes, *Kapitän*. By the way, I'm making progress. Bauer admitted you began operating off Hatteras on December sixteenth—"

"I don't want to be rude," Hedmann said, "but I don't believe Bauer admitted anything."

Shuford shrugged and went outside.

In the passageway, he motioned the guard away from Hedmann's door. In a low voice, he instructed, "Find Kesler and tell him to go through Bauer's room with two lunch trays; make certain he passes through Hedmann's room first."

With Christmas Eve twenty-four hours away, darkness fell again over the naval operating base in Norfolk, and the spotlights around the cluster of ONI buildings within the high fence flooded on at 5:00 P.M.

The lights were now lit in Bauer's room. Worn by the daylong ordeal, Bauer sat on the edge of his bed, but Shuford had not budged from his chair since the lunch hour.

"Whatever it is, *Herr* Bauer, this thing that is causing the sonar confusion, it must have been perfected within the last six months."

Bauer was silent, and Shuford reached over almost lazily to pour himself another cup of tea.

Suddenly Bauer snarled, "This is absolutely inhuman."

"But necessary," Shuford said. He glanced over at the bottle of brandy. "*Tch, tch, tch!* You haven't touched it." He reached over. "Here, let me pour you a bracer. I think we have quite a while to go."

Bauer ignored the bottle. "You've been questioning me for seven hours."

Shuford blandly shook his head in denial. "I would never do that. Six hours and fifty minutes, not counting our lunch break. Now, that is not so bad. After dinner, an hour or two; then call it a day. A productive day."

Next door, Horst Hedmann was sitting in his chair, head bowed down dejectedly. He looked fatigued, defeated. Alone, he felt he could handle almost anything, but not this way—with Bauer in relentless interrogation. The daylong ordeal had been worse for him than it could have ever been for Bauer.

Kesler rubbed his eyes. His brain felt mushy, just from listening.

"Now, since it is released from the sub—" Shuford said carelessly.

Bauer replied wearily, "Yes, since it must be released from—"

Shuford's one good eye suddenly sparkled like a diamond. He pounced. "*Must! Must!* So it is *released* from the sub. A material thing. Why didn't I think of that?"

"I didn't say that." Bauer was panic-stricken.

But his face told Shuford the mystery was cracked. It was cracked all over the room.

Shuford sat back, closed his notebook and stretched lazily. He got up slowly, not bothering to look again at the wiry sub officer. "Have a good night, *Herr* Bauer," he said, over his shoulder.

* * *

Kesler frowned. Something had just happened in Bauer's room. It was in the tone of Shuford's voice. What was it?

Hedmann arose as Shuford entered. "More progress?" he asked.

Crossing to Hedmann's table, he answered, "As a matter of fact, yes. Quite a bit of progress." He stared at the *Kapitän* for a moment, his face seemingly devoid of expression. Then he pried the cap off Hedmann's bottle.

Hedmann tried to look amused. "You could not beat information out of Heinrich Bauer. I know him too well."

"I quite agree," Shuford replied, pouring an inch into two tumblers. He passed one to Hedmann. "Drink with me," he requested. "*Herr* Bauer would not."

"I should be pleased to," Hedmann said cordially.

Shuford rotated the brown liquid in the glass thoughtfully. "You are right. A man like Bauer cannot be tortured into truth. But one sometimes may stumble on a blind spot."

"Bauer's guard is up," said Hedmann.

Shuford waved his glass at the sub captain. "*Auf Ihr Wohl*," he said. "To your health."

"*Prosit*," Hedmann toasted back.

After swallowing the brandy neat, Shuford said quietly, "*Kapitän*, I've won!"

Hedmann chuckled. "Never."

"Oh yes, I have. Tonight when you hear taps, it is not only for poor Schlisser but it is for you, and all your U-boats—"

"Never."

"I want you to listen carefully, *Kapitän* Hedmann."

"I always listen carefully." Hedmann smiled back.

"You killed Schlisser, you know," said Shuford, very quietly.

The *Kapitän*'s head was cocked to one side and Shuford marveled that there was not the slightest change of expression. "I was told that he committed suicide. I must believe what I was told."

Shuford went on, "You killed him to prevent him from talking. That was a shame. Oddly enough, Schlisser would never have talked. It is you and Bauer who will talk."

Hedmann ignored the prediction. "You must prove I killed Schlisser."

"I think I can."

"You have *not* won!" Hedmann suddenly raged.

Shuford put his glass down. "Taps tonight, and think about Schlisser . . ."

Then he left.

Kesler rose up and went off to eat, thinking about what Shuford said; wondering if the deadly game was almost over.

There was a crash on the loudspeakers resembling the slam of a door, and then Hedmann's voice ground out, "What did you tell him, Bauer?"

Honig looked up and Shuford paused to listen. He'd just entered the monitoring room.

"Nothing, *Kapitän*, nothing."

Shuford laughed softly, and tiredly. He said to Honig, "Get me the base bandmaster on the phone."

"The bandmaster? He's probably at home."

"Get him."

Shuford checked through the morning transcripts as Honig searched for the number and finally dialed it. Then he passed the phone to the lieutenant.

"Bandmaster, this is Lieutenant Clay Shuford, His Majesty's Royal Navy Reserve, temporarily attached to the Office of Naval Intelligence. Have your best trumpet player report to me in ten minutes. Building thirty-two, wing six, in the ONI compound."

There was silence on the other end of the phone. The bandmaster, obviously well along in years, wasn't accustomed to such calls at the dinner hour. "Just who did you say you were?"

"Lieutenant Clay Shuford, RNR," Shuford bellowed, "and unless that trumpet reports to me in ten minutes, with his horn, you'll find your chief stripes missing in the morning. Do you understand?"

"I gotta boy used to play with Glenn Miller. Then there's a boy—"

"Send him over immediately!"

At 9:00 P.M., Glenn Miller's ex-trumpet player stood by the flagpole in the quadrangle and raised his horn. Then the chilling notes of taps lifted toward the cold heavens, just as they had lifted every night, in that reassuring lullaby.

In his room, Hedmann listened and watched. He could see the peacoated trumpeter standing in the quadrangle, but this night the notes were so perfect that he knew Shuford had not engaged in idle talk. A fine musician stood out there, but what did it all mean? Suddenly there was a look of fright on Hedmann's handsome face.

*　　*　　*

In the monitoring room, Shuford listened, too. At the end of taps, he began to count: "One, two, three, four, five . . ."

Then Glenn Miller's boy lifted the trumpet to his lips again, and the first refrain of "*O Tannenbaum, O Tannenbaum*" came out of the silver horn.

Kesler looked out at the trumpet player. "Everybody's gonna wonder what the heck is goin' on."

Shuford nodded. "They'll wonder all night; he'll play it every hour, on the hour."

Kesler listened to the classic, glassy notes and said, "I don't get it, Lieutenant. You really think that'll rattle the Heinies?"

Shuford said, "I think it may rattle one, Kesler—a cello player from Hamburg. He has a lot on his mind."

As he was leaving, Shuford said, "I'll sleep in my own room tonight. Wake me at five o'clock."

Shuford fought the sound of the horn and his own conscience for most of the night, and then he heard Kesler saying, "It's that time, sir."

He came to slowly. "Thank you, First."

"Get any sleep, sir?"

"A little."

Shuford sat up groggily and rubbed his chin, suddenly aware that he hadn't shaved for two days. He wanted to appear fresh and neat for Hedmann, as if the whole thing had done nothing but exhilarate him. "I'd better tidy up."

Kesler asked, "You goin' for broke today, Lieutenant?"

Shuford smiled wanly. "Yes, First, I'm goin' for broke today."

He went to the washbasin and held on to it for a

moment from sheer weariness, his head bowed. Then he straightened up and splashed cold water on his face. Captain Haines was reflected in the mirror.

"I heard you had an early call, Lieutenant. So did I. All night long."

Shuford turned, resting against the basin.

"I'm ending this idiocy today. I got calls from the base commander on down. They think I'm a lunatic, letting you play 'O Christmas Tree' all night. I defended you as best I could. But you've gone far enough."

"With all due respect, Captain, not quite far enough."

"I just read your transcript on the Bauer interrogation. You let him slip by you just when you were getting good information."

"I talked to him all day, Captain. You get to know a man rather well after talking to him all day."

"Apparently not well enough to crack him. We're changing tactics on this whole thing today, Lieutenant. I've made up my mind. No more nonsense. Your relief arrives tomorrow."

"As you wish, sir."

When Haines had gone, Shuford shaved meticulously and then daubed skin bracer on his cheeks and cupped drops into his good eye. He looked very fit now, not tired at all. He showered, dressed, and went out into the passageway.

Kapitän Hedmann was haggard, and his beard was heavy. Shuford knew that he had not slept during the long hours. It was 6:00 A.M., Christmas Eve morning, still dark; and Glenn Miller's boy, still playing perfect notes after nine solo performances, raised his trumpet again.

"Stop that, stop that!" Hedmann pleaded.

"Stop what?" Shuford asked, innocently enough.

Then he stepped to the doorway and shouted toward the monitoring room. "Someone is playing a horn that disturbs *Kapitän* Hedmann. Tell them to stop it immediately."

Hedmann sat down heavily. "Thank you."

Shuford sat down across from him and proffered a cigarette, which Hedmann accepted silently. Shuford lit it for him and then said, "As you know, I spent many hours yesterday with Bauer. It was an extremely difficult day for him, you may be sure."

Hedmann stared numbly at the British officer.

Shuford continued, "Bauer was quite reticent, and you should be proud of him. You trained him well, *Kapitän*, but he did admit that whatever is confusing our sound gear was released directly from the submarine."

Hedmann bluffed roundly. "He doesn't know."

"He knows, and he talked."

"I don't believe a word of what you say."

"But you do believe, *Kapitän*. It is written all over your face."

Hedmann turned away from Shuford, closing his eyes. "My name is Horst Hedmann, my rank is *Kapitänleutnant*—"

Shuford broke through: "Bauer also told me it was electronic—"

Hedmann laughed weakly. "Now I know that you did not crack Bauer."

"So it isn't electronic. That only leaves chemical . . ."

Hedmann tried not to react; he struggled not to let the slightest change of expression come into his eyes nor cross his face. "My name is Horst Hedmann—"

Shuford said, "Schlisser died in vain. You know that now, don't you, Captain? You should have killed Bauer."

There was silence in the room for at least ten minutes and then Hedmann lifted his face to look at the lieutenant. Stricken, he said, "All last night, as you played the music, I thought about Schlisser. He'd harmed no one. Even to protect a secret, I did not have the right to kill him. I did what I believed was my duty . . ."

"The chemical, *Kapitän*, what is it?"

"I was wrong about Schlisser," said Hedmann.

"Dammit, what is it?" demanded Shuford.

Hedmann took a deep, deep breath and then murmured, "*Pillenwerfer.*"

Shuford stood up, but not with any particular triumph on his face. He said simply, "Thank you, *Kapitän.*"

Hedmann rose, too. He searched the face of the Oxford professor. He spoke slowly. "Lieutenant, the other night when you took the guards away from the rooms, did you have any idea that I would kill Schlisser?"

Shuford stared at the German officer for a moment and then walked away without answering. He went down the passageway of wing 6 to Captain Haines's office. The four-striper was reading the interrogation of the previous day and glanced up as the "Limey looie" entered.

"Now, Mr. Shuford, I want you to wind up today. Nothing detrimental on your record, of course. You tried . . ."

Shuford crossed to the captain's medicine cabinet. "Yes, I did try," he said. He opened the cabinet and took out a seltzer bottle and extracted a tablet. Then he drew a glass of water.

He heard Haines asking, "Getting to your stomach, eh?"

"Yes, sir."

"I'm sure you're actually ready to be relieved."

Shuford moved to place the water tumbler directly in front of Captain Haines. Then he held the seltzer wafer high and let it drop. It hit the water and began to fizz.

"*Pillenwerfer*," Shuford said.

"How's that?" Haines asked, very puzzled, staring at the bubbling water.

"*Pillenwerfer*," Shuford repeated. "A chemical that is released from a submarine when it is under attack. It acts like a stomach tablet. It bubbles and confuses our sound gear."

Haines leaped up from his desk, jubilant. "You broke him!"

"Yes, I broke him."

"Man, you should be happy." Haines whooped. "Merry Christmas!"

Shuford looked through Captain Haines's wall in the direction of Hedmann's room. He said, "The man in there is a tough man, a courageous man. When a noncombat man like me breaks a combat man like Hedmann, you don't feel happiness."

Shuford moved toward the door and then stopped to say one more thing. "You can try him for murder now. But never try him for lack of courage—you'd lose. And, Captain Haines, if you do try him for murder, you'd better try me as an accomplice."

Haines blinked, unable to understand all that had happened. "Where are you going, Lieutenant? Don't you want to stay here while I call Washington?"

Shuford shook his head. "No, sir. I'm going for a long, long walk."

As he passed the monitor room, Shuford heard Goldberg softly whistling "*O Tannenbaum.*" He continued down the passageway and out of the door, and then across the quadrangle in the cold dawn light. He was walking rapidly, as if he wanted to put it all behind him, not much interested in celebrating Christmas.

Kesler watched the lieutenant from the window of the monitoring room, having learned that the war was often fiercely fought with other than aircraft bombs and torpedoes or depth charges. This particular war was over, and by nightfall he'd be home and candles would be lighted and seasonal music played and the family table laden with food; but his central thoughts would be with a lonely man named Clay Shuford.